Karola Renard is a writer, editor and translator. Born in Germany, she is engaged in exploring the mythic story-lines running through her country of origin, the numerous places she has travelled and the British Isles, which she has adopted as her home. She lives in Devon with her husband and young daughter.

The Firekeeper's Daughter

TALES OF INITIATION

Karola Renard

AWEN
Stroud

First published in 2011 by Awen Publications

This second edition published by Awen Publications 2017
12 Belle Vue Close, Stroud, GL5 1ND, England
www.awenpublications.co.uk

ISBN 978-1-906900-46-5

To my grandmother, Marie Louise Ott, née Renard, who
passed on to me a tale untold

Contents

Introduction

When we speak of myth, we usually imagine an epic world of gods and heroes, of adventure and ancient lore, where brave knights slay dragons, Tristan longs for Iseult, and Parzival eternally fails to ask the one important question. When we speak of myth, we speak of great emotion, of the archetypal battle between good and evil and of a complex world that is full of symbols and meaning. In short, a world that does not appear to have much in common with your average twenty-first century life.

Yet myth is a key part of our imagination. Our immediate, uncensored perception takes place on a mythic level. We all hold a wealth of archetypal knowledge within that connects us as human beings, what C.G. Jung calls the Collective Unconscious. Mythic experience is still of vital importance to us, as it always has been. There is an unbroken fascination with all things mythic, from *Star Wars* to *The Lord of the Rings*, Narnia to Harry Potter. Such stories are tools of emotional survival in an age that transfers the structure of myth into advertising and propaganda and employs its emotional power to fuel consumerism, establish polarities and even promote war and conflict.

We think, and more often *feel*, in mythic terms all the time. We have an inherent need to make sense of our world and our own nature by creating stories of meaning. The Sufi poet Rumi wrote in the thirteenth century,

> I spring loose from the four-branched, time-and-space cross,
> this waiting room.
> I walk into a huge pasture.
> I nurse the milk of millennia.
> Everyone does this in different ways.
> Knowing that conscious decisions and personal memory
> are much too small a place to live.

Each of us knows how it feels when we step into the archetype, those moments when we feel most alive and connected with our essence, and sometimes most vulnerable. It may be when we are going through a period of transition in our lives, when we are adolescent, when we travel, fall in love, become parents or suffer the loss of a beloved person. Artists express this experience with their own unique skills. Our connection to our favourite books, music or works of art is often very important to us while we are going through such rites of passage. They help us maintain our faith in who we are and what is ahead. They may even save us from despair.

In truth, there is no divide between myth and reality. All the mythic stories of old, all sagas, legends and fairy tales, were created to make sense of people's own stories or to mark and remember a universal truth. We all have a mythic life. All of us are on a grail quest. We all arrive at the grail castle one time or another in our lives and, like Parzival, must find out what question to ask. All of us are dragon-slayers, knights, tragic lovers, princesses, witches, magicians and warriors. More often, we are fools. But if we are lucky, and keep our eyes open, we may become like the Fool in the Tarot pack who sets out on his mythic quest, ready to jump off the ledge, walk to unknown horizons and embrace change at every moment. The line between foolishness and courage is very thin, and the stories in this collection are the result of my own travels along this precarious border. They have sprung from my experiences and my deep need to make sense of what I have encountered. But they are also much more than me. They have come from a place so mystical, so deep inside, that I almost have no words to describe it.

They have come from a forest of kindling as old as humanity, from Rumi's huge ancient pastures and from the rivers of millennia. Writing these stories has helped me to follow my Fool's journey, with an open heart and mind, and the insight that my own experience is as exciting as any novel or movie. I have become a story-finder, stoking the fire of imagination at every moment in my life. Treasuring our own stories makes us Firekeepers, tending to the flame that connects us all, the flame of our imagination, passion, faith and hopes. The four sections in this collection follow the four stages of the divine feminine, whose archetypal power has been my companion for many years: Maiden, Lover, Mother and Crone.

Because I am a woman conscious about womanhood and gender, some of my writing is born from the fundamental experience of living in a female body. But my stories are, in their essence, not about gender. They are about finding a voice in this day and age when gender roles are dissolving and crying out for evaluation and a new meaning that does not create but embraces polarity. They are about crossing a sea of wounding and age-old strife, inflicted upon and accepted by women and men for centuries. They are also about motherhood, about mothering ourselves, our own divine uniqueness and holding this spark, this flame within us, through life's challenges. They tell of giving birth to one's own supreme, inimitable story. Finally, they are about keeping awake by the ashes of our failure, anxiety, grief and anguish, about scrying in the smoke of a dying fire and keeping our flame alight in the darkest places of the mind.

A story often begins with but one spark, one splinter of kindling. It is our decision alone whether we want to be the heroes, the kings and queens of our own lives. The way we feel about ourselves, our world and our future makes a difference. It doesn't matter whether we feel angry, depressed, helpless, manipulated, despairing or unloved, hopeful, adamant, compassionate, determined or connected. All these feelings are potential stories. Through our life story, our very own myth, we can initiate ourselves into the mystery of life without religion and dogma. Living our own story consciously, with a mythic and archetypal awareness, is a spiritual practice. When we give our feelings a story, we give them a context. We create a common ground that draws other people to us who will share our stories and offer their own. I believe we can reimagine our collective story. Imagination is the agency of change.

Maybe if we dare to believe in our own myths we will not be so tempted to believe in those imposed on us, the ones created from fear and control, or the ones that keep us from setting out and looking over the edge. We can look ourselves and each other in the eye, look in honesty at our suffering, and the suffering of this earth that is like the wounded Fisher King in the grail castle. If we are living and telling our story without fear, we will have the courage to probe the question it took Parzival a lifetime to ask:

'What ails you?'

The answer may be different for each of us. But whatever it is, it will come from a place of truth.

Karola Renard

Maiden Spark

Daughter of Ice

The story of the Star Maiden and the She-bear is too old to be found on the pages of written history. It is not the kind to be discovered in old libraries, since even the oldest scrolls do not tell of them. Their story begins in a forgotten valley, long before the vast lands of Siberia acquired a name. The only trace still reminding us of that story is a faded carving on a rock. Into this ancient stone an equally ancient hand once rubbed red ochre. Behind the leaves of windswept birch trees, an image of Ma, the She-bear, waits. She has raised herself on to her hind legs. Her paws are stretched out in warning, and her teeth are bared in a raw image of power. Nobody remembers her name these days, and no one has for thousands of years: Ma, the Huntress.

But many thousands of years ago the valley people knew about the She-bear's might. They would look up to heaven in awe at night and see the Huntress roaming there. Her path described the change of the tides and the course of the seasons and the clan people could tell from the shining imprint of her paws and her gleaming teeth in the dark when the time was favourable for hunting the stag and the wild boar, when songs had to be sung and when festivals had to be celebrated.

Before every hunt, the men and women would gather in front of their tents and call in the spirit of She-who-wanders-the-skies while they danced around the dying embers. They hunted the bison, they hunted the elk, and sometimes the mighty mammoth, but never did they hunt the she-bear, since it was her spirit that watched over the spears of the hunters. The valley people told each other that the She-bear had roamed the skies long before people had stepped on the soil of this land. Around their fires, they told the tale of how the Huntress had brought two children down from heaven on her back, so long ago, oh so long ago. One of them was a maiden whose limbs were made of starlight and whose long, white hair resembled grass sharpened by frost and dripping with snowmelt. Her eyes were ice-flowers looking into eternity. She was untameable and cold, and in her harmonious, motionless face was mirrored the vastness of all the heavens.

The other was a boy with brown limbs as supple and lithe as water rushing down a slope in springtime. His hair was curly and smooth like petals and his hands resembled slender roots. His face was as mobile as a nimble hare and his mouth smiled whenever he looked at the Star Maiden.

*

As they grew older, the girl fell pregnant and gave birth to a daughter. This daughter grew up in the valley, and when she reached the age when a man should come and bring gifts to her tent, her father set out to find a hunter to match her. He never returned. But one day a young man found his way to the hidden valley. When he laid eyes on the girl, he asked her mother what he had to do in order to be welcomed into her tent. The mother answered, 'Ask the mighty She-bear of the heavens to grant you success on your next hunt and do not forget to thank her when she has answered your plea.'

The young man lit a fire and danced around it and asked the She-bear in the sky to make his spear swift and strong. In the evening, he brought home rich prey and laid it before the girl's tent. And she looked at him with a smile, and she let him in.

Theirs was the first tent of the tribe that was to be the clan of the She-bear. Never did the young man forget to call in the She-bear's spirit before he and later his sons went hunting and his daughters painted their bodies and faces with red ochre and danced the dance of the Great Huntress, limbs spinning and hearts praying for a safe return. At the night fires, mothers told their children of the fierceness with which the She-bear protected her young and how she planted courage in the hearts of the hunters. And so in each generation the older women told the young how the She-bear had brought their ancestors down from the sky, and they taught them to heal illness and help in childbirth and blend red ochre for their bridal tents.

3

Only a few of the Star Maiden's descendants met with the She-bear. Sometimes she could be seen by the river, catching the leaping salmon in mid-air. Sometimes they heard her growl deep within the woods. Sometimes, when a child was born and the women gathered to call for the Huntress's protection, they were answered by a distant roar, and then the labouring woman would sink back on her bed in relief. On some occasions, blessedly rare, the women heard the echo of the Huntress's voice when the men had gone off into the wild, and then they knew that the Huntress had called the spirit of a hunter to her world of shadows. Thus the valley people lived with the turn of the seasons, and the starry image of the Huntress watched over their living and their dying.

Most children born in the valley of the She-bear were dark like their ancestor, the Star Maiden's companion. But, sometimes, one of the brown, strong-limbed women who had conceived on a cold, clear night of deep winter gave birth to a baby girl with hair like snow and eyes like the winter sky. Then the grandmothers would huddle together around her tent and hold council. They summoned the She-bear from the skies to reveal to them the name of the child that had quickened in the Sleeping Times and whose eyes seemed to look into eternity. And when the night drew to an end the grandmothers would name the newborn and tie around its neck a talisman made from the Huntress's teeth lost in the woods. Then they gave the child back to its mother until it was old enough to call in the spirit of the Huntress and prepare for a role as healer and shaman of the clan. One such girl was Snowtrack.

At her birth, the council had sat a long time. Snowtrack's grandmother had finally squatted on her small brown feet in front of the reindeer skin on which her granddaughter lay. The baby girl looked at her with wide, starry eyes.

'There can be no doubt,' the crone said. 'The Huntress has sent us a child who will be able to find her track in the skies and on the earth below, so we will never forget when to hunt for the bison, the elk and the mammoth, and when to celebrate our festivals. Her eyes are as bright as stars on a night sky and as deep as the imprint of the Huntress's paws in the snow. I say her name shall be Snowtrack.'

The other grandmothers murmured approvingly and rocked back

and forth on their gnarled calves, thanking the Huntress for her gift.

Snowtrack grew up like every other child in the valley. In no way was her life different, except that sometimes her grandmother would take Snowtrack's face in her wrinkled hands, turn it from side to side a little grumpily and look at her enquiringly. Unlike her playfellows, Snowtrack was not afraid of the peculiar old woman, who would finally let go of her and mutter something that at least sounded like approval.

'My Ama only wants to know whether I am ready yet,' Snowtrack explained to her playfellows.

'Ready for what?' the children would ask. But Snowtrack would only shrug and shake off the question the way only children can. *How would I know?* And they would run off, laughing, and Snowtrack would forget all about the whispered conversations she sometimes witnessed at her grandmother's hearth while she drifted in and out of sleep.

'In her eyes lies hidden a great quest,' Ama said to the other old women of the council who squatted around the fire. 'Eyes that look to faraway places like that must sometime be followed by arms and legs.'

This, none of the grandmothers could contradict.

*

As Snowtrack grew older, she learned to blend the red ochre and to summon the She-bear's spirit when the men went hunting. She sang and danced the ancient stories of the valley people – the same dance her ancestor had danced as he asked for the hand of the star child's daughter. She learned to be of use to women in labour, to treat all sorts of ailments and to scatter petals on the graves of those the Huntress had taken to the shadow world. Snowtrack grew tall and slender and her hair fell down her back, white as snow. When her thirteenth winter came, her grandmother died and left the clan bereft of an elder. It was then that Snowtrack left her parents' hearth and moved into Ama's tent at the camp's fringe to take her place in the council of grandmothers.

That summer, one would often hear discontented chatter among the She-bear's clan. There was many a young hunter who watched

Snowtrack's withdrawal with regret, and many a woman who shook her head that such a young maiden should be made an elder of the council. Snowtrack was little bothered. She gathered herbs of healing as she had done since her childhood. She blended the red ochre, and tanned skins that she then painted with curious patterns. She freshly covered her grandmother's drum and proudly wore the bear claw given to her at her birth.

'A grandmother of thirteen winters!' Snowtrack's mother said to her companion. 'It is as if ice crept down the mountains in summer and the rivers flowed upstream. Never has the Valley of the Great Huntress seen the like! How can my daughter help the women in labour when she has never lived through the pain of giving birth herself? How can she blend the red ochre for our dead when she has never buried a companion or a child? How can she understand the women's dread if she has never loved a hunter and never had to fear for his life? I do ask myself whether the grandmothers have decided wisely.'

Snowtrack's mother was not the only one in the valley who had doubts. Now that Snowtrack lived in the elder's tent she was the first of the grandmothers, and like them she resided alone, without children or companion, and lived off what the clan people placed in front of her tent flap. And although her ice-flower face, her hair like freshly fallen snow and her considerate manners earned her the grandmothers' trust, her body always gave away her youth.

*

Two winters came and went. Spring saw the hunters trekking to their summer camp and roaming the tundra. With the falling leaves they returned, as they had done since the beginning of time, and brought their prey back to their companions and the children of their hearths; and when the snow melted they set out again. The women tanned skins and fished in the spring creeks. They fell pregnant and gave birth and sometimes they buried a child in a wrap made from otter skin. From her tent, Snowtrack watched over the rhythm of life as her grandmother had taught her. Her voice, sometimes deep and guttural, sometimes high and shrill, summoned the Huntress's spirit when danger threatened. She knelt in front of women writhing with labour pains, murmuring soothing words, swaying on her heels to the ancient rhythm of becoming and passing, and lamenting silently when a child of the bear clan had set out on their last hunt.

Only one thing was different: since Snowtrack had begun to carry the staff of the elder, none of the valley people had heard the roar of the Huntress. Her elder sisters had long since taken companions and given birth to children and yet they seemed much more childlike than Snowtrack, who had been made a grandmother at thirteen. The people respectfully made way for the maiden elder who walked steadily through their row of tents, but in their gaze lay something else, some deeply rooted doubt, and fear lurked behind it. The bear clan sensed a change, sensed it like cracks in their coarse vessels, slowly eating into the clay and splitting open the carved patterns. Something came creeping from the steppe like a predator through the grass and lurked in the shadows cast by the mountains.

As the third summer passed, the days grew shorter and the people gathered in their tents and listened to the darkness outside. There was more than one among them for whom the stillness outside told of death and foreboding. In the past, the tribe of the She-bear had often told the story of their ancestors, the star children. This winter, no one spoke of things past, for they were full of worries about what was to come.

It had not been a good hunt that summer. The hunters had brought home a woeful bounty: five young hunters had lost their lives tracking down the meat that would have to tide the tribe over the Sleeping Times. This winter, no children were born and many of the elderly died, some of the grandmothers among them, so the council became, all of a sudden, very small. Many a gaze wandered towards Snowtrack's tent at the mountain's foot, and unkind thoughts went with them.

Snowtrack's mother gathered her children and grandchildren around the fire and knitted her brows.

'What are we to do?' she asked her companion. 'I am the mother of the council's elder and the daughter of she who came before her. Does my daughter not see the suspicion following her? The valley lies sleeping, none of the women is with child, and many a hunter

7

has set out on his last hunt too soon and will never share his bed with a companion. I ask myself, has the Mighty Huntress left our valley? What will become of us if no children are born into our tents? What can it all mean? Never has our valley seen such a baleful summer. What are we to do?'

Her companion looked at her with a frown, and her daughters squatted on the reindeer skins and said not a word.

'My companion,' the old man said, 'you are brave and strong and have given life to many children in this tent. You will be a grandmother of the council soon yourself. You have given birth to a star child, an image of our ancestor from the most distant of times. Have you so little trust? Did not the roar of the Huntress give you courage every time you were in labour?'

Snowtrack's mother hung her head for a moment, but then replied, 'You are right, my companion, she is of the star children, but did not her eyes look away from here, into the distance, even at her birth? And is her face not motionless like ice, her skin cold like melting snow? The grandmothers say she is the guardian of the Huntress. But I say she lures winter into our valley.'

Snowtrack's father shook his head. 'Winter, my companion? Much sooner ice and frost will enter our camp in the wake of vicious thoughts like yours.' But the ice that soon started creeping down the mountains towards the valley seemed to mock his words.

*

One morning in late summer, when the leaves had not yet started to change colour, Snowtrack was roused by a sudden frost in the air. She found the skins of her tent covered in rime. The ground under her bare feet was frozen solid and a thousand fine splinters of ice hung on the wind, got caught in her hair and melted there. Snowtrack sheltered her eyes with one hand and looked out over the plains to the distant mountain tops. Their caps of ice had swallowed the wooded slopes. Snow rested heavy on treetops hardly visible under their load. Dark clouds chased over the steppe, over which the ice spread, almost gently, like a hunter covering his bride. Snowtrack's keen hearing caught the sounds of frightened animals breaking through the woods in the distance. In the valley below, the clan stirred, and she heard the first sounds of surprise that quickly turned into cries of dismay. Snowtrack looked to the horizon, and it was as if the ice desert greeted her as a kindred spirit. She found her voice and sang a deep-throated song, a song as old as ice itself. Then she crept back into her tent and began beating her drum.

'Come, grandmothers, come!' the drum sang. 'Come to hold council, and come fast!' And the grandmothers came. They squatted on brown heels round the fire while the land around them slowly fell waste. When they had all gathered, Snowtrack stepped into their midst. 'The starry sky has frozen,' she said, 'and the land below is dying. Already the image of the Huntress is barely visible. I can hear her calling from a great distance, and she is vanishing away. Soon she will be silent. We must leave this valley, if we do not want to lie down in a grave of ice.'

The grandmothers looked at her with huge, earnest eyes and one after the other limped down to the tents to hurry along their children and grandchildren. Snowtrack stayed behind alone and clutched the bear claw at her neck.

Ma, she silently called, *Ma, you have predicted a quest for me. I see it has begun. But I can barely hear your voice anymore.* And dread crept into her heart in the same merciless rhythms with which the ice slowly covered the valley.

*

The clan folded up their tents. They tied their belongings to their backs. The children, who at first had run around their parents in excitement, quietened down and sat on the hastily built sledges, wide-eyed and silent. Like all the others, Snowtrack scattered red ochre on her frozen hearth to bid it farewell and wrapped herself in her warmest otter-skin cloak. She took her fishing spear, her satchels with herbs and her staff of bones which she carried as the clan's elder, and she left the camp without looking back. The clan greeted her with silence. Only the grandmothers, sitting on the sledges and holding the young ones, nodded to her and gave the sign for departure.

It was a desperate procession that followed the trail out to the steppe. In the sounding stillness spread by the ice, Snowtrack heard the women quietly weeping and listened to the distraught children asking questions. Before they left the valley for good, Snowtrack rubbed red ochre between her palms and painted the silhouette of the Huntress on to a rock with her fingers. Then she took her staff and led the way into the empty white plain.

They followed the fleeing herds. A pale winter sun hung low in the sky till the early dusk made it hard for the hunters to find any tracks in the snow. The women cut holes in the frozen rivers to catch some fish but they were soon too weary and their spears became slow. They ate dried meat and sour berries that made their lips split and bleed. Their faces grew grey and empty and ribs started protruding under their skin like a tent's frame.

Rarely did the hunters bring back meat from their excursions. Just sometimes they found the carcass of an elk that for a short time brought back strength. In every shadow, predators lurked, roaming the desert of ice as hungrily and as desperately as them. Sometimes when they woke up in the mornings, one of the hunters who had been guarding the camp at night was missing. Then Snowtrack would be the only one who lamented him with the ancient chants, while his companion and children watched her impassively and eventually turned away. Snowtrack walked ahead of the clan and left them every bite of food she could spare. Behind her, she would hear the sonorous murmur of the grandmothers calling to the She-bear shrouded from their sight in the heavens. But one after the other, they, too, fell silent and were laid in graves of snow. And still the desert of ice stretched onwards to the horizon.

Days ran together and it was impossible to tell how long they had been wandering. Snowtrack searched the skies for the image of the Huntress every morning but saw nothing but clouds and mist. Many of the elderly and young members of the clan had embarked on the longer journey and now it was nearly only hunters and their companions who sat around the fires at night. One of Snowtrack's sisters and all of her children too had been left behind on the steppe. Snowtrack had, as custom demanded, sat down at a fire of her own come evening. But the fewer fires lit each evening, the more her people moved together and sought comfort in the closeness of each other.

Hunger and exhaustion were outweighed by the hopelessness that settled down with them by the fires each night. One evening, even Snowtrack stepped into the ring of people gathered round her father's fire and warmed her freezing hands. The clan made way for her, but at the same time a hostile murmur arose. She looked up into the gaunt face of her mother, who pensively weighed the white staff of bones in her hand. The others held their breath, for only the clan's elder was allowed to touch the staff passed on by their ancestors, the star children. Snowtrack rose and wordlessly stretched out her hand. The fiery glow flickering over the snow tinged her pale skin the same colour. Tiny ice crystals glittered in her hair, and her bright eyes faced the staff in her mother's brown hand. The expression in her beautifully carved face was as unreadable as ever.

'Look at her,' said Snowtrack's mother slowly. 'Look at her standing there. Our clan's elder, our guardian. With eyes like ice-flowers and skin like snow, as if the ice desert itself had given life to her.' The clan stared at Snowtrack as if seeing her for the first time. Some hissed in agreement and edged away from her.

'Look at our guardian,' her mother said. 'Snowtrack was what I called her, as the elder, my mother, instructed me. The track of the She-bear in the snow she was supposed to find. But she turned out to be useless. With her drum she has called the ice into our valley and with her songs she has shrouded the image of the Huntress from our sight.'

The clan again hissed its agreement, louder this time. Brown hands made gestures of distrust, and the people began to form a circle around Snowtrack as she stood there tall and lithe and white.

'My companions,' Snowtrack's mother said, 'the day she moved into the elder's tent I said that sooner would ice creep down from the mountains into the valley than a girl should become a grandmother. We have offended the Huntress by choosing one unworthy to lead our clan. Since she moved into Ama's tent, no one has heard the call of the She-bear. I tell you, this girl will lead us to our death. We have been blinded and now the Huntress's rage pursues us with this never-ending winter.'

Snowtrack still did not move, though the circle around her grew tighter and tighter. Her eyes were locked into her mother's. Silently

11

she stretched out her hand again. Fear and anger fought in her mother's face. She looked down at the staff in her hand, then back into Snowtrack's motionless face. Then she raised one knee and broke the staff of the elder in two.

In the breathless silence that followed, Snowtrack slowly lowered her arm. She did not make a sound, but her shoulders stooped a little and the old proud tension left her body. Slowly, reluctantly, one after the other turned away and sat down by the fire without looking at her. When Snowtrack's mother left the communal fire, dragging her aching bones to settle down at Snowtrack's own fireplace, the girl wrapped her otter-skin coat around her body. She paused to touch her father's shoulder as he stared into the embers. Then she left. Her father raised his head to watch her go. He saw her long shadow twitching over the ground for a moment before it became one with the darkness.

*

Snowtrack wandered alone under endless skies in search of the Huntress's tracks. She was the only living creature in a world gone void. No track, no disturbance by man or animal tarnished the cold cloak under which the hunting grounds of Snowtrack's clan lay hidden. Huge snowflakes caressed her face, mocking her loneliness, and then dripped as icy water from her hair. *Maybe the ice desert has given birth to me, as they say,* a voice whispered in her head. *And I must wander this dead land until the darkness is complete and there will be neither earth nor sky. But if I be a true daughter of ice, why am I so afraid?* She kept walking until at last her legs gave way and she fell into the snow.

She did not feel the cold that had so long cut into her limbs. The sky above her joined with the lifeless land and became a spiral of churning white.

Ma, Snowtrack thought, *Ma, do not desert me. From when I began to think, I have felt you pulsing in my blood and singing in my dreams. Now I have lost your track and your children have cast me out. This winter has made my heart freeze, and only emptiness is in me and around me. Maybe your time has run out and you have returned to the far skies where I cannot follow you. If you hear my call, Star Mother, then come, come and do not let your children die un-*

der the ice. She closed her eyes and fell asleep. And dreamt.

Fragile and lucid was her spirit while life left her body. In her dream she saw the few survivors of her clan huddling together at the edge of a dark forest. A cold wind chased over the plains and the ice crystals glinted under a waning moon. But for the first time since she had set out on her quest the skies were clear, and there, there was the image of the Huntress looking down on her children. The dreaming girl drifted deeper into oblivion, listening to a soft echo, the sound of life, hidden in the womb of the earth. Between her fingers she felt not snow but wiry, warm fur that gave way under her clasp. The warmth crept up her arms and she felt herself being lifted up. Between her legs she felt the same delicious warmth and the movement of hard muscles, stretching with every leap. A strong back arched underneath her in a rhythm as old as the earth. Wind roared in her ears as the She-bear carried her across the plains, and Snowtrack listened to the comforting snort that went with each leap. She listened to it for a long time, and for a long time the mighty paws scratched over ice.

The landscape lost its contours under the Huntress's wide leaps. The mists started to part. A suddenly clear night offered the view of a forest edge fringed with fires. Snowtrack looked up and saw the same waning moon that in her dream had lit her clan's most recent camp. Its light danced in shining patterns on a vast ocean that stretched out as far as the ice desert behind her. Black waves licked at the shores as if to warn the exhausted people not to come too close. The Huntress slowed down and finally came to halt with a low grunt, her ears playing attentively. Full of wonder, Snowtrack followed the She-bear's gaze. At the black water's edge a bridge of ice led into the unknown beyond the moonlight. 'There,' the Huntress's twitching ears seemed to say, 'there lies your track.'

*

The clan roused from its restless sleep. One after the other sat up and fearfully looked around. One after the other struggled to their feet. The air was yet icy, but the heavy wet fog had vanished. They huddled together and looked hopefully to the night sky. Every pair of eyes was searching for the same thing: the constellation of the Huntress. Finally, Snowtrack's father voiced what none of them was willing to believe: 'She is gone.'

Truly, the constellation was nowhere to be seen. The silence that followed echoed their shock. The elder, Snowtrack's mother, began a shrill lament. The wind carried her desperate cries over the steppe, all the way to the black water's edge, where a girl and a mighty she-bear listened without moving. When the cries died away, the Huntress turned and trotted in the direction of the soft wail that was all that remained of the clan's hope. The girl followed her broad tracks through the snow.

It was Snowtrack's father who saw them first. He tugged at his companion's cloak, not gently. The woman, crouching on the ground, did not look up. Only his prolonged nudges made her lift her eyes. She heard the She-bear before she could make out her contours against the trees. A deep murmur trailed along the forest edge, then crescendoed in a roar as the Huntress threw back her head and announced her return.

The clan knitted closely together. The few survivors stared at the She-bear rising on her hind legs. They had believed her to be watching over the clan's fate since the beginning of what was yet to be called time. Now she had stepped down from the skies, so real and so elementally full of life that the people did not believe their eyes.

'Has the Huntress come to lead us into the longest sleep?' Snowtrack's mother whispered in awe.

Nobody answered her. They just stood, silenced. And Snowtrack stood equally motionless, and waited.

She felt the Huntress's vigour resounding in her own exhausted body, felt the strong muscles at play. And she understood. The veil of not-knowing tore. Earth and sky fell into complete symmetry. Her lonely quest had brought her to a place within where all causes, sorrows and fears were stripped of their meaning. In her dream, she had listened deep down into the frozen earth. And softly, very softly, an answer had travelled back to her through the frozen womb of soil. So softly whispered the secret life within that only the dreaming girl could hear it. It was a spark so fractional that it could survive darkness for only the blink of an eye. But it was still there, and

14

Snowtrack remembered. The same spark within her had sung this new life home. A tingling, drunken joy hummed in her blood. So alive, so persistent. She had been initiated by the infinity of life. She had cast all her trust in the balance. And she had been heard.

Had her surrender conjured the She-bear from the skies? She did not know. But fearlessly she stepped into the circle and sang what she had been blessed with, sang it in a guttural voice, sang for the Huntress and her might, sang for life sleeping under the ice, sang for a dancing spiral of birthing and dying, coming back to where it had begun.

Her clan crowded around her, still silent, and listened. This night, Snowtrack sang under a clear sky, and the Huntress watched over her from the shadows of the trees. As a dirty dawn crept over the ice, Snowtrack's mother squatted down at her daughter's feet. The girl stooped and helped the older woman to her feet. 'Come, grandmother,' she said. 'We will go and find a place where you can sit in council with the elders, as befits your age.'

*

They travelled over the bridge of ice. Snowtrack led them along the edge of the black water that stretched out endlessly on both sides. They needed their last resources. Holes, painstakingly hacked into the ice, allowed them every now and again to catch some fish. The Huntress followed them at some distance. At night they would make out her silhouette against the clear, starry skies. They did not have fires anymore and could hardly sleep for cold, but the presence of her huge body comforted them. They dragged themselves along. Snowtrack walked in the lead, always carrying on her shoulders one of the children whose mothers could not find the strength to carry them. The Huntress kept watch so no one was left behind. And after several days wandering the frozen ocean, they saw land.

It was Snowtrack's mother who beheld it first. A narrow touch of brown on the horizon, gradually becoming broader. After another two days, it had grown into a shoreline fringed by rocks and woodland. The air became warmer. On the third day, they saw waves breaking against the bridge of ice, and that night they did not rest but wandered on. The fifth day, they lit a fire on the shore and watched the seagulls drifting in the wind, welcoming them with their bold, tuneless song. To the people of the bear clan, it was the sweetest thing they had ever heard.

*

Snowtrack blended the red ochre and painted her face and thighs with new symbols birthing from within her: they were whirls, spirals, waves, images of life. She painted the image of the Huntress on the rock and, dancing, mimicked her sturdy pace. She sang until she lost her voice. At last she allowed her spirit to rest as she had learned from her grandmother and sent it out to search for the Huntress. The She-bear came from a cave in the rocks and snorted a friendly greeting. Her bright, starlit eyes were a perfect reflection of the girl's own. Snowtrack thanked her silently for the gift of life. The mighty animal stood motionless and held the girl's gaze for a long time. *It is time*, her eyes seemed to say.

Snowtrack returned Ma's gaze; it was the silent understanding between two friends who were of the same kind. Then the girl hung her head. 'I know,' she whispered. 'But I find it so hard to leave them behind. They depend on me, will continue to depend on me, on somebody.'

Ma snorted softly and came close, breathing warm air against the girl's cool skin.

I will take care of them, her voice resounded in Snowtrack's head, *as I always have. Follow me now, Daughter of Ice. You are not of this place anymore.*

Snowtrack felt the truth of this deep within, in the body she no longer owned, in the body she had left behind when she died in the ice. A spirit body now, the edges of which tugged and pulled her, wanting to pass on to another world. She placed her hand on Ma's warm, strong neck.

'So be it then,' she said. 'Where are we going?'

'To where we have come from,' the She-bear replied as Snowtrack climbed on to her back and held on tightly. 'Both of us.'

The last thing Snowtrack heard as Ma set off, with a single mighty leap, were the delighted cries of her clan from their camp. She knew that the Huntress's image had once more appeared in the sky.

When the first child of the clan was born beyond the desert of ice, the women who kept awake in the labouring mother's tent heard a muffled roar the wind carried from the ocean's edge. Snowtrack had been the last descendant of the Star Maiden, her ancestor. After the clan of the She-bear had crossed the bridge of ice, there was never again born a child with eyes like ice-flowers and hair like meltwater.

*

Long after Snowtrack had laid herself down in the ice for the longest sleep, a clan girl came to her grandmother one night. She had spotted a most curious star in the night sky, a star of icy blue light that outshone all others.

'There is a star in the skies,' the child said, 'so beautiful and clear like rime.'

The old woman looked up to the panoply of stars and nodded her approval. 'This, my girl, is the brightest star in the winter sky. We call it the Daughter of Ice. There, in the north, she keeps watch.' The old woman held out her arms as the little girl scrambled into her lap. Then she continued with her tale:

'They say she lights the way back home for hunters who got lost. Some even say she once lived here among our people. When the Great Ice suffocated all, she alone set out to find life in the ice desert, and her spirit brought it back to our tribe. From her, we learned that, in truth, life knows no death. She reminds us of it every night. You see?'

She took the girl child's hand and turned it upwards, and slowly, very slowly, painted a spiral of red ochre into her palm.

The Firekeeper's Dance

The healing maiden shall return,
and from her footsteps
fire shall spring.
The Prophecies of Merlin

In a land of endless savannah and wide skies, a land that is called Kenya today, there once lived a girl called Randa. She had sultry eyes and long, harmonious limbs that glowed in the sun like the black ebony masks her father carved. The men of her tribe smiled when she passed by them, carrying her water jar, for Randa was a beautiful sight to behold.

She was a daughter of the threshold, neither child nor woman. Her body already gave a promise that her soul could not yet fulfil. The day of her moon blood had not yet come and, in many a lonely hour, Randa's soul searched for her old lightheartedness. She seemed to have lost it somewhere between the long walks to the waterhole, preparing the food, sweeping the hut and caring for her younger siblings.

Often she would ask herself what being a woman was really about and why all the girls of her own age were so keen to be given to a man. They giggled and whispered by the waterhole, adorned themselves with beads and bangles and braided their hair into tiny plaits. But even though Randa could see the beauty in her tribe's young men, who had strong supple limbs and the easy stride of a panther, she did not feel she wanted to belong to any of them. There was something yet missing, something she had to understand, something like a tangled yarn that needed unravelling before it could be used for mending. Randa did not know what her soul was yearning for, and so she sometimes felt confused and sad. She wished she could be allowed to dance again.

Randa had always loved to dance, had loved it more than any-

thing else she knew. From when she was a tiny girl, she had been
drawn to the sound of the drums and had joined the men who
danced between the huts, their bodies twirling through the dust. She
heard the clapping and stamping over the drums' bewitching song
and her blood began to heat up until her heart was beating in her
throat. She would dance then herself, to the adults' amused looks.

They would say to one another, 'Look at this Randa and how she
dances! Never has one seen a girl dance like that. Look how she
dances the flight of birds in the sky and the leopard in the high
grass!' And they would shake their heads.

Randa paid no attention to them and danced the circling birds,
the soothing rain, the burning sun, the antelopes' swiftness and the
predators' velvety ease, and even the spear dance of the young warriors. She danced the south wind's hot breeze. She danced when the
ground was cracked from heat and drought and her calves were covered with yellow dust. She danced in the rainy season when the
dense curtain of water turned the dust into mud that welled up between her toes and splashed up to her hips. Randa was happy when
she danced.

But as she had grown older and reached the threshold of womanhood, the elders had forbidden her to dance. 'Randa,' they had
said, 'Randa, daughter of the threshold, you are too old to dance in
this way. The only dance you may dance in future is your wedding
dance, before we bring you into your husband's house. Until then,
you should cast down your eyes, for the power of dance is too
mighty for young girls, and the gods do not look kindly upon those
who don't obey. You must not risk the gods' scorn, young Randa
with your eyes like embers, for if you do they will punish you and
your life will be hard and bitter. Let the men dance the gods' songs.
Go back to your grandmother's hearth. You will tend the fire there,
for it seems you need to learn how to keep your own fire in check.
Tend it well, so it does not burn us all in our sleep! Forget the trance
of dancing, Randa. Forget it quickly, or we will find a way to make you
forget it, a way that is not as gentle as your grandmother's.'

With a heavy heart Randa returned to the hearth fire that day.
She squatted down beside it, let her forehead rest on her arms, and
her tears fell on to the embers, hissing in desperation. The rising

smoke wrapped itself around her face, but instead of burning her eyes and taking away the air to breathe, it covered her hot, wet cheeks like a soothing balm. She caught a deep, spicy scent. As she looked up, the dying flames seemed to twitch expectantly.

Randa hurried to stoke the fire, and the growing flames danced just the way a woman would sway her hips at her wedding dance. In the fire Randa saw the form of a woman, and a face of red swirling flames seemed to smile at her.

'Who are you?' Randa asked, puzzled.

The firewoman lazily swayed her flaming hips and said in a voice as warm as the fire, 'Don't be afraid, little Firekeeper. I am what was and always will be. I am old and new. I have been born and I have been buried. I am Ma, the earth you walk, the fire you keep, the water you fetch from the well and the wind that stirs your yearning. I am a spiral dance, the shadow hunting your soul and the healing light in which it finds rest. I am every song that has ever been sung and the drum's eternal rhythm. Do you not know me? Have you not danced my song many times?'

And Randa's heart remembered. From then on, she loved tending the fire. She would often speak to Ma, who patiently tried to answer her many questions. Randa's grandmother began wondering why her unruly grandchild had suddenly become so tame. She would watch the girl who sat by the fire for hours at a time, staring into the flames as if they held the secrets of all creation. But the old woman did not complain. She let Randa carry on, for she knew how hard it could be to be a daughter of the threshold and to have a home neither here nor there.

Randa was astonished by Ma, who constantly changed and would appear in a different form every time Randa looked into the flames. Sometimes she was a long-legged young girl with high breasts like Randa herself, sometimes an old crooked woman with grey woolly hair and gentle eyes like Randa's grandmother. At other times she was curvaceous and wiggled her broad hips. But always her stories were wise and her words loving. In such a way, a year went by.

On the day when Randa finally stepped into the house of women, she squatted in front of the fire and her belly ached with the unfamiliar cramps as her first moon blood flowed. Ma looked at her with a mixture of pride and compassion.

'So you are a woman now, little Randa. I know it hurts, but breathe in and listen. Now you are growing into the power to create, to give birth and to sustain. Your blood is a sign of eternal change, giving life, taking it again, turning the spiral. Are you ready now, my little keeper?'

Randa nodded and the pain eased a little.

'Why do you live in the fire, Ma?' she asked. 'Why are you not where the men dance the rhythm of life? Do you not rather belong there?'

Ma shook her fiery head. 'I live in this hearth fire because your tribe has forgotten me, Randa,' she said, with only a hint of sadness. 'Only a few still know my name. I have long since lived in oblivion. And there I must remain unless your people remember me. I cannot reach out for someone who does not want to see me. This is why I do not live in your world, for there is nobody now who will dance my song.'

Randa looked at her with wide eyes. 'But you are so powerful. How can you choose to be in exile if you could force the people to see you?'

Ma smiled and shook her head again. 'No, Randa Firekeeper, this is not my way. Don't you understand? I am you, and you are me. We are one, if you choose it. I am the spirit at home in my children, but only you can make me visible. Will you bring me back, Randa? Will you dance my song on the village square for all to see?'

Randa cast down her eyes. 'I dare not dance, Ma. I am not allowed. What will I do if the gods punish me for my feistiness? I am afraid. You should have chosen another girl, for I have become a coward.'

At these words, Randa's searching soul that had been at peace for some time began to weep, because it knew that Randa had spoken the truth of others. Ma looked at her for a long while, her flaming features full of love.

'Don't be sad, little Randa. I wish you understood, after all this time, that you do not have to fear any manmade gods when you are with me. The day that you feel that the voice in this fire is in truth your own, call out for me and I will come.'

With these words Ma vanished, and from that day on Randa searched the embers in vain. Her heart was heavy with grief, but her fear of the elders weighed heavier.

Now that Randa had stepped into the house of women, it did not take long before the elders came to announce that they had found a husband for her. The village's sorcerer stood in her grandmother's hut and declared that the gods had pointed out the young hunter destined for Randa. The girl sat by the fire, eyes cast down, and did not say a word. Her soul had fallen silent and she felt numb and empty. Her grandmother, who worried about her, let her drink the freshest water and gave her fruits to enjoy, but the girl continued to gaze into space and avoided meeting anyone's eye.

On her wedding day, Randa's grandmother braided the girl's hair, adorned it with tiny beads and rubbed fertile clay on the soles of her hands and feet. It was then Randa finally looked at the older woman and asked, 'Grandmother, did you know that Ma of the Thousand Names lives in your hearth fire?'

Over the old woman's lined face passed the shadow of an old memory. In her kind eyes, for a moment, Randa could see the reflection of a dancing flame.

'So you too kept the fire of the threshold?' asked the grandmother, and sadly the old woman shook her head. 'And you, too, have finally decided as I did when I stepped into the house of women.' She put her hand on her granddaughter's cheek. 'Now Ma must wait for another girl to be her keeper. Until then, my hearth will be a desolate place.'

The old and the young woman stepped out into the hot day and left Randa's youngest brother to watch the fire. When Randa, beautiful as a velvety summer night, greeted her husband the drums began to beat for her last dance. Randa began to sway with their rhythm and danced the wedding dance as she had seen so many women dance it before. She danced and danced and was drawn into the magic created by her own moving body.

She did not see the men look at her with desire and how the women began to clap to the rhythm of her twitching feet. Between Randa's hip bones a warm, fiery light slowly began to spread. Her stamping feet drove the drummers into a yet wilder beat. The fire spread further and took her over, flooding her limbs with light, and she raised her arms to the sky. And then she wasn't dancing the wedding dance anymore, but something wild and ancient, a dance that none of the watchers had ever seen before. It was a dance of red hot passion and trembling flames, a dance so untamed, fierce and beautiful that it echoed in the soul of every man and every woman. Randa danced with devotion and trust, and her husband, the drummers and all the tribespeople were stunned to see Ma of the Thousand Names brought into their midst.

But then, unexpectedly, the tribe's sorcerer jumped into the circle that had formed around Randa, and pushed the young woman to the ground. The spell was broken, the people withdrew in shock and the old man began to beat Randa with his staff. He cursed the girl with every stroke until she was lying at his feet, bleeding and sobbing. Her husband-to-be stood motionless, his face frozen. Only Randa's grandmother tried to come to her aid, but the onlookers held back the old woman. Still the sorcerer's staff was striking down mercilessly, but Randa had stopped sobbing and pleading and now lay very still.

Only when a child's dismayed cry suddenly rang from within the cluster of huts did the angry old man cease to beat the girl at his feet. Smoke was rising from the hut of Randa's grandmother and flames licked at the thin wattle-and-daub walls. Panic broke out as the villagers ran to try to put out the fire that threatened everything. The dryness of the season and the huts' thatched roofs worked against them. Soon they all ran from the place of destruction, carrying what goods they had managed to save from the flames.

Randa was still lying unconscious where the sorcerer had left her. From a safe distance the villagers looked on as the flames grew into a curtain of fire. Some would say, later, that the fire had eaten up their village with the easy grace of a dancer. Amidst the fire, Randa did not move. Some men held on to Randa's grandmother, who fought them with all the remaining strength her frail body could muster, trying to run back into the inferno to save her grandchild. Randa's husband-to-be took her younger brothers by the hand and turned his back on his bride's destiny.

Had he not turned away so easily, he might have been witness to something that would live on for ever in the minds of his people.

As the flames reached Randa and began to eat away her clothes, the girl slowly sat up and stretched out her arms in greeting, as if to welcome a favourite friend. The flames danced up her arms and enveloped her like the tender touch of a lover. Then they suddenly fell away again. From the spot where her tribe watched the scene, Randa's grandmother stopped her desperate wailing as she saw that her granddaughter was back on her feet and had begun to dance again.

While all around her the remains of her village burned down, first to glowing embers, and then to ashes, Randa danced amidst the raging fire. Her feet stamped the earth that was as hot as a forge. Her arms reached lovingly for the clouds of thick smoke that grew denser and denser until the girl at last vanished from the sight of her people.

Afraid of what they had witnessed, the tribespeople sought refuge in the wide savannah and did not return for many days. Randa's youngest brother, with tears of distress in his eyes, admitted he had fallen asleep by the hearth fire while everybody else had been celebrating his sister's wedding. Finally Randa's grandmother set out with the sorcerer, Randa's husband-to-be and a few others to the place where their village had once stood. Nothing was left of the huts that had been their homes. Everywhere, between the crumbly debris, new grass was growing in the cracks and crevices. Where the hut of Randa's grandmother had been, there was a single fire burning in the hearth.

When the sorcerer saw this, he cursed quietly and staggered away, back to the tribe's camp, muttering angrily to himself. Others were fearful as well, and not many dared to return to settle in this place. The few who did, though, worked relentlessly until a new cluster of huts stood in the place of ruin. When they had finished their work they celebrated the new life they had been given with food, drink and the sound of drums. The men danced until their bodies glistened with sweat and then turned yellow with dust. And on the other side of the village square danced the women, swaying hips and stamping feet, and they sang a song about the girl who had given them back their voice.

There were some among them who were daughters of the

threshold and about to step into the house of women. And although they were of an age where they were at home neither here nor there, they did not feel it, because they did not dread the journey.

Brighid's Flame

Mairi was descended from a family of bards that was as old as the island on which she was born. The island lay on the edge of the western ocean. The bards called it Éire, the Abundant One. In the south, emerald green valleys sloped in gentle terraces towards the sea, while in the north a harsh wind chased up and down the cliffs and ruffled the gorse bushes that, besides the purple heather, were the only dabs of colour in a landscape shaped by peat and fen.

There, in the northwest, Mairi was born, escorted by the seagulls' laughter, at a time when winter was slowly melting into the sea. All that day, the village that cowered between the cliffs and the sea listened to the singing that came out of the cottage of Mairi's parents. It was Mairi's mother who sang. She sang in an ancient language that flowed across the moors in strangely entwined patterns and rhythms: at times loud and shrill, at times heartbreakingly gentle and sad. Her songs told of fishermen and farmers, of love and loss, of hope and trust. Everything the green island had seen come and go, everything awakened and blossomed softly with the labouring woman's song. She sang against the pain, sang against the never-ending contractions and against her rising fear because the child would not come. It took a day and a night before Mairi finally came into the world, and all this time her mother's singing did not die. The last song begged St Brighid for help.

'Come,' sounded the voice of the woman in childbed, 'Brighid, Sovereign of my hearth, softener of all hardship, white maiden of the land, come to me and bring this girl into the world.'

It was the small hours of the morning, and stillness was spread over the village. The women who kept awake and trembled with the labouring mother thought they heard a soft tingling, as from tiny silver bells, until finally the cry of a newborn made them sigh with relief.

The little girl was christened Mairi, after the Mother of God, and she sang before she learned to speak. She learned the songs from her mother and the ancient stories and myths from her grandfather, who was a master of the gracefully curved harp. When Mairi was not helping her father and the other men with the boats she would sit for hours at the old man's feet, cheek resting against the instrument's smooth frame, and feel it vibrating when her grandfather every now and then accompanied his tales with an absently played melody.

Thus, life at the edge of the cliffs went on. The villagers did not get much news of what happened where the ocean ended. The island had seen many conquerors come and go. The invaders had come from beyond the sea and rarely penetrated into the heart of the island, where they only found an ancient, treeless landscape with deep lakes and gorges and, finally, another ocean, stretching out infinitely into the west.

Hundreds of years ago, intruders had come from the icy north and landed on the southern shores with their swift dragon boats. They had raided, marauded and engaged in fierce fights with the island kings. But as time passed they had stayed, had made peace and built ports and trading posts. The same happened to those who followed in their wake. Soon the invaders found themselves entwined in the island's magic; they forgot their language and the traditions they brought; they lived with women deep rooted in the island's soil and thus became part of the land that welcomed them with its lush, curvy abundance and its Janus face of wind, turf and salt. Many different clans lived scattered there: fishermen, traders, seafarers, farmers and shepherds, each with its own stories, kings and laws. Thus, the island had formed its people from the beginning of time and in its primeval majesty had never submitted to the laws of foreigners.

But then, some thirty years before Mairi was born, a new king from the neighbouring isle sent his soldiers. They spilled off their boats like a never-ending stream of ants. With their number and their heavy armour, they covered the island and left their strongholds like septic boils on its body. Many clan kings died in hopeless battles opposing the intruders of iron and the fire that flew from their muskets and canons. They fled into the west and hid in the high moors' mists and rough mountains. There, they kept the island's age-old heartbeat alive with their songs and stories, while in the east the soldiers hunted down the bards and poets, banned their language and forced the people to live by rules that were meaningless to them.

For Mairi, born at the edge of the western ocean, this news of oppression and death for a long time remained only a story shared in whispers by the fire, nightmarish admittedly, but as remote and unreal as the traditional songs and artfully twisted verses had already become for the people of the south. Mairi's Clan set great store by the seclusion that secured their safety and shielded them from the eyes and ears of foreigners. And so the occasions when visitors came to the village were equally as rare as those when one of the villagers left to attend to some business in the nearest market town.

On a tiny archipelago in the bay stood a cluster of windswept stone cells that were inhabited by monks. Solitary pilgrims they were, whose travels had at last brought them to the end of the known world, where they had met God in the storm and the rhythm of the waves eternally leaping up the cliffs. The villagers adored these humble, earnest men and often supplied them with food and small offerings. There, one evening in early summer, Mairi had her first encounter with Brighid.

She had crossed over with her father, taking advantage of the sea, calm for once, and for the first time entered the tiny church where the monks had gathered for their daily prayer. There, where the wall formed a niche, a statue made from coarse stone was visible in the twilight. It was a woman, a girl still, whose right arm was raised as if in benediction; the other was draped over the back of a cow, whose udder was swollen and who was rubbing her head trustingly against the girl's shoulder. From both sides of her body a pair of wings stretched out, encircling the animal in a manner both protective and awe inspiring. At the girl's feet a snake curled, its head watchfully raised. Behind her, barely visible in the shadow, the almond-shaped eyes of a wolf guided Mairi's eye to the graceful lines of his beautiful yet dangerous face and his tail curled around the winged one protectively. Next to the wondrous winged girl, in another oriel, Mairi recognised the image of her own patron saint, the confidence-inspiring figure of Mother Mary holding the holy child.

'Who is this other woman?' she softly asked her father, but he only put a finger to his lips and reminded her to be quiet and not to disturb the monks in their prayer.

Lost in contemplation, Mairi regarded the figure with the strange animal companions. In the church's half-light the contours of the stones became blurred, and the little snake seemed to move, while the big, soft eyes of the cow swam in the candlelight and glowed. Mairi suddenly felt her soul reaching out, and an unfamiliar yearning mingled with the monks' singing.

When Mairi asked her mother about the images of the winged girl, she ruffled her daughter's hair and adopted a thoughtful look. 'It is the Lady Brighid, little Mairi,' she said. 'It was her I called upon when you wouldn't come into the world, and she sent me her snake of healing, so we could both live, you and me. I saw it, a snake white as freshly fallen snow, here at the foot of my bed.'

Mairi thought of the snake curling at Brighid's feet and asked, 'But if it was Brighid who kept you safe, why did you not make her my patron saint?'

Her mother slowly shook her head. 'Brighid is the daughter of the morning, the heart and soul of our land. She is the white cow of abundance, feeding us, and the grim wolf of protection, guarding us from the soldiers. Her fire keeps our hearth safe from harm. If she wants you, child, she will choose you, no matter what your name may be. The land chooses its bards, warriors and priests according to its own wisdom. Thus it has always been, and thus it will remain, as long as the sea licks at these shores.'

'And you, mother?' Mairi asked. 'You and grandfather, do you also guard the land and the sea with your old songs?'

Her mother smiled. 'I certainly hope so, little one. With every song that is forgotten, a piece of this land must die; or so they say.'

'Then surely there must be stories about Brighid? Can you not tell them to me?' Mairi besieged her mother, still excited by the image of the girl in the church which had seemed so alive.

'Stories there are many, Mairi,' her mother smiled, 'and each has its time. Have patience. Brighid has brought you into this world, and now you have met her again. Maybe there is a particular fate waiting for you, daughter of my heart. If she calls you, you will find her story and it will become your own. Listen!'

Mother and daughter held their breath and listened to the thunderous song of the waves.

'Listen,' the mother whispered, 'and you will hear her voice sing in the wind, and every cow you milk will nourish you with her grace.'

With these words, she returned to her work and for once they remained the only answer Mairi was granted to satisfy her questions. She did not quite understand what her mother meant by the land that called people to its protection the same way a chieftain gathered his warriors and bards around him, but she was enough child of her island to sense the truth behind her mother's words and to trust that one day she would also understand their meaning.

She played among seaweed and flotsam, crusted with salt, and listened carefully to her grandfather's songs in order not to miss the occasion if he should take it upon himself to sing of Brighid. Sometimes she dreamed of the delicate figure of a young girl whose bright almond eyes regarded her with the same intensity as that of the stony wolf in the chapel. One evening she felt as if the twilight was playing pranks on her. She thought she could make out the fleeting silhouette of a girl behind a rock. For the blink of an eye, a pearly laugh hovered in the air, to be swiftly replaced by a wild swan's strident cry. For a moment, the proud bird hung motionless over the cliffs, then it flew inland with a regal stroke of wings.

It was her grandfather's stories and tunes that satisfied her curiosity a little. They told of a light-bearer, a maiden who rose in the morning to light dawn's torches on the hills and who at eventide guided the cattle safely back to their shelters. Then her mother would sing of a wild swan that flew over the land and lent words of magnificence to the mouths of poets and bards, escorted by the sound of a thousand silver bells. Mairi watched the bards of her clan gather and shake a silvery branch of birchwood adorned with tiny bells, thanking the Lady Brighid for the words and melodies that flowed from their instruments and their hearts.

The monks on the island told her of a holy woman who, a long time ago, when the God of the Christians had come to the island, had given her miraculous belt to a poor woman so that henceforth she could heal and feed her many children. Mairi heard of a dainty white cow with ears red as flames who wandered the hills in the morning dew and vanished as quickly as she had appeared. She listened to a song about a white wolf that led astray the foreign soldiers who tried to hunt him down, finally lulling them into a magical sleep from which they awoke only years later. She heard of a young mistress of the forge who on a red hot anvil forged the souls of the people while the embers hissed and spluttered of the hardships and bitterness each life held.

But most of the stories revolved around the flame. Brighid, so they said, guarded the flame of life, the fire that was the quiet embers of age-old rites and the exuberant sparks of poetry, a light that gave birth, nourished and warmed and that kept vigil in every hearth on the island. In Mairi's heart this flame formed a glowing promise that one day, she hoped, would be redeemed.

From time to time Mairi visited the image of the swan maiden on the monks' archipelago, and in the crystal nights of late winter, when the day of her birth returned, she lit a tallow candle for the daughter of the morning who came to the frozen earth and sang it back to life with a silver rod.

*

When Mairi was about to leave her childhood days behind, soldiers came out of nowhere and abruptly cut what should have gently unfolded. In Mairi's memory the events of this day merged into a swirling spiral of fire, violence and death. It nested below her heart and would make her wake up even years later, sobbing with horror. Mairi had never known cruelty. But that day it washed over her like a spring tide and ripped her soul from its safe place, dragged it into a world of blood and fire and left it there without shelter. Her parents died that day, her grandfather, her three siblings and two of the eight monks on the archipelago. The tide of violence reached her father, and the other men, at the boats they had not been able to launch quickly enough. Her mother and her sister had been gathering driftwood at the beach. Her grandfather she later found in his cottage, next to his shattered harp. Her brothers, chased down by two soldiers, lunged themselves off the cliff to which they had fled. Their chieftain, stripped and chained, his hair cropped off, was forced to watch helplessly while the soldiers set fire to the boats, cottages and warehouses.

Mairi was on a solitary excursion along the cliffs when she saw the smoke rising in sticky clouds. Something burst in her head, a cry born of unbearable pain, like the death scream of a tortured animal. It bred, multiplied, until her insides sounded from the agony of the land beneath her feet, from the pain that reached down to the deepest roots of the earth. She ran until she reached the village, where a grotesque silence was an inexplicable counterpoint to the shrill ringing in her head. She found her mother and her sister; she found her father. She dragged her grandfather from his burning cottage.

Her world ended then. She walked through a gate and on the other side comforting emptiness awaited her. Mairi dug her family a grave of sand. When the monks crossed over the next day to bury the dead, she was gone.

*

She wandered the moors blindly, the wailing behind her forehead growing into a tuneless lament, sometimes shrill and desperate, sometimes merely an exhausted sigh. It drove her on, through brackish water, undergrowth and brown hills, away from the ocean. At night she curled up beneath the gorse bushes and slept a cold sleep, paralysed and void of dreams. She ate what little she found on her way and avoided the hamlets and cottages. They belonged to the terror in her soul. But the smoke rising from many of them told her that there, likewise, death had visited. She became gaunt and hollow-cheeked and over her eyes fell a veil beneath which images from the otherworld drifted. She caught misty glimpses of the realm of ghosts and shadows, where her parents' souls tenderly touched hers, feathery and fleeting, before they glided back into eternity.

She did not know how long she had been travelling between the worlds when she saw the wolf. That night she had lain down to sleep and cowered on the cold earth when her restless eyes were caught by a patch of light. There, in the blackness, sat a dainty white she-wolf, haggard and shaggy, but with eyes as bright as the moon above. It looked at Mairi steadily and the girl sat up and stared back in fascination.

Its fur seemed to reflect the moonlight and exuded a soft glow that reached all the way to Mairi's bed and embraced her. Girl and wolf regarded each other for a while, and then the animal rose, strangely awkward, and trotted off. Mairi saw that it was hurt and one of its hind legs was dragging feebly behind. After only a few painstaking paces, the wolf stopped and turned back to Mairi. Its golden eyes pierced the veil that was spread over the girl's consciousness, and Mairi scrambled to her feet and followed the wolf. They wandered under a dark moon, crossing the still plains, and the numbness in Mairi's heart made space for the memory of a wolf carved from stone, lying at the feet of the swan maiden.

She followed the white wolf for many nights. She avoided the roads where the soldiers travelled and cut across country. In the day she slept and when she woke at dusk she felt the she-wolf's intense gaze on her. It hurt her to see it limp, because in spite of its calm and gentleness Mairi sensed that it was in great pain. The silvery glow that surrounded it grew fainter every night. Mairi forgot her own grief, so concerned was she for her new companion. It was as if she felt the sharp pain in her own tired limbs. The landscape through which wolf and maiden travelled began to change and, gradually, the gorse-covered mountains stood back behind wide open valleys and fertile meadows parted by a broad stream. Mairi did not know where her companion would lead her, but the she-wolf was the only thing that tied her to her lost life, and so she followed it, and did not ask.

Under a clear starry sky Mairi laid eyes for the first time on the ring of closely standing lime trees. In their midst she intuited the shrine more than she really saw it. She became aware of a flickering light that swiftly darted across the trees and every so often flashed the leaves with a warm golden light. A fire burned within the grove, a fire that promised warmth, a fire that beckoned and welcomed her. Mairi's enchanted eyes were hooked by the dancing colours, warm reds and soft golds. When she finally turned and looked for her companion, the wolf had vanished. She called for it, but it had melted into the darkness of the branches that nearly reached to the ground. She was perplexed. Slowly she felt her way down the slope, passed through the ring of smooth trunks and eyed the twitching shadows playing in front of her feet. In the clearing stood a small stone shrine wherein burned a fire. The whitewashed walls were covered with artful paintings, their curls and twists only just visible in the darkness.

A soft wind whispered through the grove and made the flames leap momentarily. Two slender lime trees marked the entrance. Their heads bowed towards each other and formed an elegant leafy arch over the shrine roof's ridge. Mairi stood very still and took in the wonder of this peaceful place. The wind stroked her tired legs and carried with it a silvery tinkle that sounded familiar to her. And there, under the lime arch, stood the delicate figure of a maiden whose contours seemed to blur before Mairi's eyes. The girl's hand rested on the tree to her left, and her long, silvery blond hair shimmered through a thin mother-of-pearl veil that concealed her face and reached down to her hips. She held out her other hand and invited Mairi to come closer. Unable to avert her gaze from the apparition, Mairi felt a great tiredness come over her. As the white maiden turned and entered the shrine Mairi realised that she walked with a limp that made her appear strangely broken. Her bare feet left bloody stains on the immaculate white stone.

Mairi woke up to the sound of voices, only reluctantly emerging into consciousness. As she opened her eyes she looked into the lined face of a very old woman who was regarding her attentively. The crone was all dressed in white and her hair, snow white like her dress and thinned by age, was spread over her shoulders like that of a maiden. Mairi turned her head and saw that more women, all of different ages, stood around her in a circle. The youngest, squatting on her heels next to the crone and watching Mairi curiously, was little older than Mairi herself. All the women wore the same simple white dress. The hair of each of them fell unbound down her back in a similar maidenly fashion. All of them looked at her with the same benign attention.

Mairi propped herself up on one elbow and blinked into the grey morning light creeping through the lime trees. She lay on the chalk floor in the middle of the shrine, next to a stone basin in which glowed faintly the embers of a dying fire that one of the women was just now reigniting.

'She is awake,' enthused the youngest girl with obvious excitement.

The other women smiled and looked at each other in amusement. The crone stroked Mairi's hair, her eyes taking in the weariness and the loss that had brought Mairi to this wondrous place.

'Don't be afraid, little sister,' the crone said. 'Your journey ends here.' Turning to the other women: 'Today is a day of joy. Our number is complete again. Bríg has brought us a new keeper.'

That day, Mairi became the youngest keeper of Brighid's flame. They were nineteen, Bridie the next youngest, merely two summers older than Mairi; Sian the eldest, a crone with a frail body and a quicksilver mind, a grandmother of fifteen. Each of them, so they told Mairi proudly, had been chosen by Brighid and had answered the cry of the swan, some very early; some, like Sian, only later in life.

Some had been guided to the shrine by their longing to serve, some by a happy coincidence and some by hardship or bitter loss, like Mairi. They were a sisterhood of keepers and guarded Brighid's flame, the heart of the island, which burned within the white shrine in the clearing and was as old as the land itself. Long ago, bards and harpers lit it in honour of the ancient goddess Bríg to mark the festival of the melting snow. But one day, at the time when the first followers of Christ came to the island, there had appeared a brave girl with healing hands who carried the name of the goddess: Brighid, the 'bright one'. She was a chieftain's daughter, but when she grew into womanhood she left her family and brought Bríg's abundance and healing from her father's hall to the poor, the sick and the oppressed. Many sought her out, many Christians among them, and she willingly shared her knowledge of Bríg's flame and its creative power with everyone who was a true seeker. Many women came to Brighid's cell and sat before the flame the wise woman kept there. Some stayed for ever.

Many stories told of the miracles that had happened through Brighid's hands and the suffering they had eased. She had been the first of the sisterhood of the flame and, with her companions, had built and guarded the shrine. Countless women had followed them since. Some said it had been the ancient goddess Bríg herself who had renewed her shrine through Brighid the recluse and had called to her service the Nineteen Keepers whose task it was to never let die the flame that burned in the stone basin.

Thus Bríg and the saint who carried her name became one in the memory of the people. Their descendants lived and worked in the little retreat close to the shrine for centuries, they gave praise, they fed off the land and they looked after as best as they could the sick and hungry who came to them. And every night one of them kept vigil next to the smooth, round stone basin that held the flame. On the twentieth night, the shrine remained empty, for on this night, so the keepers told Mairi, the saint herself watched over her flame.

Mairi donned the white robe of Brighid's keepers, and on the nights of her watch she sat next to the fire with her heart full of devotion and thanked the swan maiden with all the reclaimed ardour of her soul for the refuge she had found. She still felt fragile, at times nearly transparent and crystalline, easy to break, and often fatigued, but in the flame she had found a consolatory presence. It was very soft, like a faint lingering note from her grandfather's harp, but it wrapped itself gently around Mairi's fearful being and slowly brought healing. Here, in Brighid's shrine, Mairi experienced a love and devotion so deeply rooted in all life that her body sometimes seemed inadequate to hold it. More than once she felt that her boundaries would dissolve, that she would melt into her essence and become one with this grove around her, at times gentle and mellow, at times ecstatic, but always full of life.

She saw the same mystery in the faces of her sisters and knew that she had been touched by greatness. Slowly, slowly, she was able to let go of the terror that had settled inside her. She tried to comprehend it by dressing it in songs and poems, and wondrously beautiful words she found. Thus Mairi became a bard. She learned to play the harp like her grandfather. In just this way the flame grew in each of the keepers' soul, and each brought it to the world in their own unique way. Brighid nourished patience, tenacity and pluckiness in her young, vigilance and care in the mature and the wisdom of the mystic in her eldest sisters.

At Brighid's great festival on the cusp of spring, people came from the surrounding villages and brought offerings for the shrine and the sisterhood. There they danced and played and sang and listened in awe of the youngest keeper's harping. They felt as if they could hear their sovereign Lady laugh like a breeze, brushing the chains of a thousand silver bells that adorned the shrine that day. They felt life rising in their hearts and loins and thoughts.

From Bridie, who had soon become her accomplice and friend, Mairi learned to write her songs and stories down on parchment. There were a few heavy books in the retreat which Mairi could barely carry on her own. Within their pages, she found the voices of those who had come before her. She was deeply touched every time she was able to add a song of her own to the wealth already contained there. She marvelled at the fresh ink seeping into the pages long gone yellow with age and began to understand. Here Bríg's ancient wisdom lived on, hidden and protected, while the soldiers tried to drive her spirit from the hills, moors and dales.

For a long time, Mairi had denied any thought about the conquerors, so remote was the terror in her memory here in her peaceful shelter. They belonged to a time of which Mairi did not ever wish to be reminded. But beyond the grove of lime trees suffering grew. There pillage reigned, and violence. There destruction trailed over the land, followed by unheard screams. The people's fear increased and began to paralyse the land.

*

As the years passed, the sisterhood withdrew more and more into seclusion. Rarely did one of them leave the shrine and its surroundings if there was no immediate need. When they went to a deathbed or a lying-in, they went after dark. Their visits were hasty and secretive and they learned to be on guard at all times.

The farmers were forced to give away a part of their harvest to the soldiers, and so they were famished even before winter came. The sisterhood hungered with them, since they had always been supported by the community and shared the harvest with the people who worked the land. There was barely enough to feed the cattle and poultry and no surplus from their vegetable plots to exchange. The sisters also lacked wood for the shrine. Bridie and Mairi often went to the nearby hills to dig peat for the fire and returned freezing and hungry to a sparse meal and a cold bed. But the keepers resisted the bleakness surrounding them as best as they could. They gathered to pray in the shrine and endeavoured to trust, but the people's bitterness and despair made wide circles, and hunger did one more thing.

Shortly before winter solstice, in Mairi's nineteenth year, old Sian fell ill, lay down on her bed and did not rise again. Mairi spent long nights at the bedside of the crone who had been mother, grandmother and teacher to her. She fed her strong teas to soothe the spasmodic cough and sang for the old woman when the she dozed off.

'Little sister,' Sian said fondly while she struggled to lift herself up to drink the tea. 'Tonight is your watch. Will you pray for me at Brighid's fire? I wish the Lady would send her snake to escort me through the gate and to show me what lies beyond.'

Mairi looked at her sadly. 'When she calls you, sister, you will be the last that needs anyone's pleading. Your journey will be cheerful and without pain. I only wish it would not be so soon. The shadows close around us, and Brighid's flame withdraws into oblivion. The soldiers drive out our knowledge with torches and muskets. We need you, Sian, and your counsel. There are decisions to be made. What will become of the books and the sisterhood come the thaw? Without you, we will be at a loss.'

Sian shook her head slowly and was shaken by a soundless spasm that threw her back on to the narrow bed. Some time passed before she was able to speak.

'My time is up, Mairi. It has been a long and wealthy time and I have done my best to fill it as the Lady asked of me. In my time, there were no soldiers and oppressors. Now I am old and the time that is to follow belongs to you, little sister. May the Lady mark my words, I do not envy you. It is a time of war, of death and fear, and it grieves me to see what has become of this land and that it has to be your battle, my girl, for you have lost so much in your life already. But she has called you, and it is you she has to rely on now, not me.'

Mairi had wrapped her arms around herself. A tear ran down her cheek and fell on her hands unnoticed. 'What was the point of her bringing me here,' she said, 'of healing me, only for me to see her defiled, treated with contempt and forgotten? Once I thought she was so strong, that nothing could truly harm her. But when she is driven from her own lands and jeered at, then everything loses its meaning and soon we will stoke nothing but an ordinary hearth fire.'

Sian's eyes were closed. The papery lids fluttered from the exertion of speech. 'You are right, my girl. With mockery and oblivion, her presence fades. She only has a voice as long as we give it to her. This is the only meaning you may allow times like these. The tapestry of her wisdom grows thin and worn, everywhere holes gape and only a few threads are firmly entwined. I say, each of you be one of these. Sing against oblivion, Mairi, write down what has been passed down and do not let the flame die. It will be few that see you, but each that does is another thread in the tapestry. And maybe there will be a time when many hands again will take it up and tie on and weave new patterns. Maybe some ornaments will be lost for ever, but wherever an echo of her voice can be heard people will remember.' A new spasm shook Sian, and she gasped for air in vain.

Some of the other women had come closer to hear the old woman's last words. Young Bridie covered the crone's tormented body with another blanket.

Sian looked briefly into the strained faces and in each she read the same fear. 'Be on your guard, sisters,' she whispered. 'Take good care of yourselves and weave in hiding. Nothing is won when you stand against a maelstrom of iron men whom you can't resist. Be ahead of danger and never be seen by those who wish you ill. Throw your voices into the wind and let them drift down the rivers. Be in the whispering leaves and in the spluttering hearth fires. Bring Brighid back home to her lands.'

She groped for Mairi's hand and squeezed it faintly. Then she fell asleep. The keepers silently looked at each other. With the quiet unity that can only thrive in a community held together by years of common work and devotion, they gathered closer around Sian's bed and bid her farewell.

As darkness fell, Mairi set out for the shrine. This night, she heard the long-drawn-out lament of a wolf in the distance and she knew that the days of the shrine were numbered. In the cold grey light of the morning, she put one of the last, precious logs in the fire and left the shrine to bury Sian.

*

The day of Brighid's festival of the melting snow, they distributed the belongings of the retreat, the heavy leather-bound books among them, and prepared to leave the shrine as Sian had suggested.

'Let us go in pairs,' Mairi suggested. 'Then the journey will be less lonely and we can look after each other if one of us falls ill and can't fend for herself.'

The other women agreed.

Two elderly keepers decided to stay at the shrine. 'As long as we can keep the flame, we will stay,' they said. 'We have spent the better parts of our lives here. We are too old to go on a journey so harsh and arduous.'

Mairi laid her hands on their shoulders. 'Then we thank you,' she said, 'for your loyalty and your bravery.'

One of the crones shook her head, streaked with grey. 'No, little sister. I fear it is not bravery that keeps us here, but fear of the unknown. It is nothing to be proud of. From now on, our prayers will rest with you. The Lady protect you and keep each one of you safe.'

'Then you will be the centre of our tapestry,' Mairi said and embraced them. 'And may Brighid hide you from the sight of the soldiers.'

Thus, the keepers of Brighid's flame separated and were scattered to all the four winds. Mairi took her harp and went with Bridie, who carried on her back some of the heavy leather books in which generations of women had shared their knowledge and experiences of Brighid. They wandered far and wide and sought shelter in the cottages of farmers and fishermen. Nearly all of them welcomed them with friendliness and listened to the tale of Brighid's shrine. Bridie's stories and Mairi's songs brought consolation and sometimes laughter and joy, but the two young women were constant witnesses of the thraldom forced upon their countrymen and the cruelty it brought.

One time, they stayed with Bridie's clan in the island's eastern woods. They found barely half the number of people that Bridie had left as a child when her father had brought her to the shrine. What they found instead was abuse and assault, and the people paralysed by so much violence. Their tale of Brighid was greeted with respect, but the spark could not grow into more where people had become strangers to their own land and their own songs and traditions and when even their ancient language, the language of their poetry and wisdom, had been taken from them.

Another bitter winter passed and another spring found its way back to the lands of Brighid the Forgotten. Mairi and Bridie had no news of their fellow keepers of the flame. Life and service at the shrine slipped further and further into the distance, the memory of the beloved daily routine and the community of Nineteen faded, until only a vague feeling of loss remained as the last connection between the scattered members of the sisterhood.

The daily struggle for food and shelter left little room for the pain. In some ways Mairi was grateful for that, though she knew that each day was only a delay and she dreaded the abyss of hopelessness that lurked behind each moment of leisure. And so they wandered through the short summer, following the mighty river into the west, retracing, without knowing, the journey Mairi had undertaken years ago on her own. They fled the conqueror's grip and spoke of Brighid where people were willing to listen. As the days grew shorter again they ventured far into the west and reached a great lake on which islands drifted like swans, played about by long-fingered trails of mist.

They found shelter with the clan that lived on the lake's shores, who welcomed them with a surprising enthusiasm. 'Our bards and harpists', the chieftain said with blatant pride, 'have been blessed with Brighid's grace ever since we can remember. Long time ago, at the festival of the melting snow, when the bards of the island gathered and challenged each other in contest, it was ours that brought home the greatest fame and were graced with the Lady's silver laugh. So you are most welcome, sisters.'

Mairi nearly cried over those words out of sheer gratitude. For the first time in endless months, she thought she could feel Brighid's presence. 'We thank you,' she said. 'We thank you so much.'

They asked him for news of the sisterhood and whether he knew what had become of the last two keepers who had remained at the shrine, but he shook his head. 'We live here very quiet and solitary and since the soldiers have come we stick to ourselves even more. We hear little of what happens in the east these days.'

Mairi understood; the people hid in the enchanted solitude of the wide marshes and lakes the same way Mairi's own people had tried to withdraw to the harsh cliffs and the sea.

The two women slept at the lake clan's fires and were granted the chieftain's protection. The clan's dwellings formed a loose line around the shores of the lake. When the mist rose from the water at eventide, it flowed over the slope to the thresholds and seemed to open a door into the realm of dreams. It was a gentle, otherworldly place full of poetry, only permeated by the cry of waterfowl and the songs with which the fishermen rhythmically dipped their oars in the water.

During those first days and weeks, as the frost slowly began to paint icy flowers on the ground, Mairi would often sit at the shore and watch the swans gliding by, their long necks gracefully arched. She was overwhelmed by the beauty of this place where every hard line and every sharp edge had been smoothed by water and mist. Small wonder, thought Mairi, that in this place many poets are born. It was the least masculine place she could imagine, a place of intuition and not of the mind. She could already sense the winter revealing the bones of the land that now lay frozen and silent. Huge flocks of crows swept over the fields and stripped away what little was left to nourish man and beast.

The timeless and dreamy landscape comforted her in a way. Since the night old Sian had died, Mairi had not met her soul guide, the wolf, but on these shores every living thing seemed to speak of Brighid. It was a place of withdrawal, a rare bastion of the old ways, and this made Mairi feel bitter as well as grateful.

Many hours she sat there and fought her contradictory feelings. A sucking, numb despair twisted her insides. She felt as if this world was drifting off into the mists and taking her with it, away from the soldiers, away from the shrine and the flame that she did not even know was still kept alive. The web she had promised to weave hung from but a few thin threads. She knew that she could not keep wandering, winter after winter, hungry and cold and unable to do more than sing of Brighid who, to most, had become a mere spark of memory. But to settle meant to be silent. Day in and day out, Mairi listened to her soul and waited for an answer. Only emptiness echoed back to her.

Shortly before winter solstice, Bridie returned from a nearby hamlet where she had traded fish for woollen blankets. Her face was pale and her eyes huge with horror. She brought the news of how the shrine had met its end: the grove razed, the flame extinguished, the two old women – last keepers of the flame – found in pools of their own blood. It had taken a long time for the news to travel to this part of the island. The ashes were now long cold and the last keepers laid to rest in unknown graves. Mairi's eyes fixed on the bale of cloth behind Bridie's saddle. Its ochre red blurred her sight and became a swirling sea of flames that filled her whole vision. She saw her clan's village burn once more and she heard once more the banshee-like screaming in her head. Before the wall of fire her mother's eyes appeared, staring emptily into the sky. Bridie, tears running down her cheeks, tried to take Mairi's hands. Mairi only shook her head, turned and went down to the shore. The thunder in her head shut out the shrill lament started by the clan women to honour the dead keepers. That evening on the shore, at dusk, something tore apart inside Mairi. The blackness that had so long waited behind the dam wall of her will flooded her inside and finally broke through. And Mairi, who never in all her life had raised her voice in anything other than praise, wailed in pain. She let the unsung lament of old ring out across the waters and sang a mad keen for Brighid, soul of the land, who had deserted her and left nothing behind but dead space.

The beauty around her no longer held any comfort for her. With the lazy stroke of a swan's wing, the beauty of Brighid's legacy glided away until it was swallowed by the mists. Mairi followed the huge bird into the shallow waters and kept wading. The cold made her draw breath sharply. She began panting from lack of air and sudden panic. The lake took her in and purged the despair. As the ground disappeared under her feet she fell backwards and for a moment looked up into the frost clear sky.

Take me with you, Lady, she thought. *Wherever you have gone, don't leave me behind.* As she began to sink, her hand hit something leathery. The blade of an oar found its way under her armpits and lifted her. Firm hands took her around her waist and dragged her into the curragh, where she fell down, gasping. The eyes that looked into hers tied a new thread into the torn tapestry that was the memory of Brighid. Mairi awoke the next day on the isle of swans.

*

'A dream voice in a dream land,' Mairi said to Sencha. 'This is what I am. Sometimes I feel as if I were made of glass.'

The bard smiled. 'When I look at you now, you seem fairly solid to me.'

Mairi echoed his smile with a new-found calmness. 'I am an echo from the past, of which only incomprehensible lines reach the real world.'

They sat on the jetty in front of Mairi's cottage on the isle of swans. This time the bard had brought her not only supplies but also the news of Bridie's wedding.

Since that winter night, more than a year ago, when Sencha had drawn Mairi from the waters and had brought her to the isle of swans in the middle of the lake, she had seen Bridie only one more time. The older girl had rowed over to her friend's curious new retreat. Bridie had not asked her to come back, but her eyes, which had always been so ready to laugh, mirrored Mairi's own deep helplessness. They sat in front of the lopsided hut of reeds and watched the swans glide past. Some of those who had already formed an attachment to the leftovers of Mairi's meals apprehensively stretched their necks towards the two women.

They were silent for a while before Bridie said, 'I wonder whether it has all been a dream in the end. The shrine, the keepers, us. Nothing seems to be real anymore. Neither our journey nor what we once were. I know I have given a promise' – she wiped a tear off her face with the back of her hand and did not look Mairi in the eye – 'but I have forgotten what it is about.'

Mairi reached for her friend's hand. 'Go home, sister,' she said gently. 'Go back to your woods and your clan. And if you can, remember from time to time. And if you can't, forget. She will always know where to find you.'

For the first time in all the years she had known Bridie, Mairi saw her become truly angry. 'But she is gone, Mairi. They have driven her away with their hatred. And they destroy everything that remains of her. It is not enough, don't you understand? It has simply not been enough. We are too few.'

As they embraced to say farewell, Bridie said, 'Be safe, sister. I wish I could be brave and stay with you.'

Mairi returned the embrace fiercely and for a moment more clung to her friend and last confidante, the last thread that tied her to her life as Brighid's keeper. 'No, Bridie,' she whispered. 'You don't need courage for that. It is only that I am as afraid of life as I am of death, and so I must stay here for the time being, between the worlds, until I find an answer.'

Bridie kissed her cheeks one last time before she entered her small curragh and left the lake and Mairi for good.

*

Mairi explored her little island where waterbirds nested and the reeds bowed down under the weight of the morning dew. She started to build a more substantial dwelling and bound the heavy leather books into oilcloth that Sencha the bard had brought for her from the mainland. She remembered her childhood skills and made a boat from tar and skins, a fast and nimble curragh like those which the fishermen used on the lake and those her own people had set out with upon the ocean.

She went fishing with spear and net and sometimes hunted rabbits along the shores. During her first winter on the island, many wolves sneaked around the lake, their bright eyes twinkling through the reeds, but none of the hungry animals approached the solitary huntress roaming the marshes. Months passed during which Mairi spoke to no one but Sencha. Her harp she had left in the bard's care, and he provided her regularly with everything she needed and could not procure or make herself. She bathed in the stillness of winter, and as it grew warmer she really did swim, diving into the clear waters and the song of the birds returning from their exile.

Every morning through the winter, she got up and went about her newly invented daily routine, and yet part of her constantly sought for meaning. She ate, drank, repaired the roof of her dwelling and built a shed for her boat. She began to fall into the same timeless rhythm as the other beings living on the lake. As winter yielded she was so completely drawn into its laws and ancient cycles that, slowly, the tormenting questions fell quiet and lost their urgency.

The peace she had found was not the gratefulness and deep healing she had experienced at the shrine; it was an armistice that would allow her to survive and to find her way back to the place of stillness and eternity within herself that Brighid had shown her long ago. Sencha was soon a natural part of the tranquil rhythm she had submitted to. He was a quiet man with a calm, firm way of moving and bright eyes whose colour changed according to his moods, like the ever shifting play of clouds across the sky.

During the cold winter months, his visits were short. They did not speak much as he warmed himself at her fire before making his way back over the frozen lake. Though blessed with the gift of music and poetry, neither was very experienced in the exchange of mere courtesies. And so they found a suitable arrangement in each other's silent company and neither of them felt obliged to interrupt this routine. What they had seen of each other, in the moment when the greatest agony of Mairi's soul had lain open before this stranger as he had pulled her into his curragh, made it even less needful to waste words. Sencha had understood. He was the first new thread in Mairi's tapestry, the first to begin to repair the torn fabric. She saw it in his eyes, and she trusted him. After a while, they began to talk. As the lake thawed, Mairi told Sencha about her life at the shrine and the promise she had given to old Sian. A promise she had been unable to keep.

He told her of his own visit to the shrine. He had been a child at the time, long before Mairi had arrived to join the sisterhood. He had listened to the contest of the bards and had heard something resembling a silvery laugh, filling the air like the tinkle of bells, as his grandfather sang the praises of Bríg, the bright one, who had made the poet's mind a shining vessel of truth. Sencha's words brought back with clarity the enchantment of the shrine. Here was another who had not forgotten.

When one day in spring Sencha told her about Bridie marrying a man of her clan, she felt glad and relieved. She understood that this was her friend's way of easing her burden instead of rejecting it. She said this to Sencha, who smiled at her in his usual cautious way.

'For some people the love of another is the tar that saves their curragh from sinking,' he said thoughtfully. Then he looked at her with a distant expression on his face. 'But not for you' he added. 'Not for you.' And, more softly, 'and not for me.' He turned away and fetched from his boat the supplies he had brought for her.

Sitting on the jetty's rough timbers with her knees drawn in, Mairi lazily let her hand trail through the water. 'What then?' she asked pensively, speaking more to herself than to the bard. 'What does it need then? I have never found out. If I had, I suppose I would not be here.'

Sencha, whose back was still turned to her, straightened himself, shielded his eyes from the sun and looked over to her. She watched his guarded, upright figure.

'A gift of grace,' he finally said. 'A certainty that whatever happens will, in the end, again lead to where it started and nothing will be truly lost. The very thing you are here for.'

Mairi wrapped her arms around her knees and rested her chin on them. 'I once thought I had found it,' she said. 'Back then, when Brighid brought me to the shrine.'

'Yes,' the bard said. 'I too thought I owned it. Until the day I pulled you from the water.' He regarded her face for a long moment, then smiled and turned away again, nimbly wading into the shallows. He pushed the boat from the jetty and raised one hand in farewell, but did not look back. He would still come and visit her every now and then and remained a loyal friend, but from that day on they avoided such conversations.

*

May came and the sun drenched the lake with lazy contentment. One morning Mairi awoke to the heron's cry and found the surface of the lake painted with all shades of gold. Something in her tight-

47

ened with an unfamiliar yearning. She wanted to stretch out her arms and greet this new feeling, wanted to grasp it, own and understand it, but with the force that filled her also came restlessness. And it stayed. At night she lay on her bed, more connected than ever with the life rustling and whispering in the reeds and moving over the waters in unseen, ever changing circles. Everywhere life celebrated its return while Mairi lay alone, yearning, and did not know what for.

In one of these drunken summer nights, he came to her. She heard his curragh, ever so gently touching the shore, heard a bird's startled cry, heard the water lapping around the poles of the jetty and listened to his soft footsteps. And then she saw him standing in the doorframe, a tall shadow against the moonlight, and neither of them spoke a word of greeting. He took her in his arms, his own yearning reaching out for hers, and as they embraced she trembled in a frenzy of new sensations. Night became an endless melody, pouring from a wind harp formed by their entwined bodies, echoing widely across the waters. The whispering breeze stroked their flesh and smudged out all opposites until they became one great song of praise. Finally, it cooled them as they exhaustedly huddled against each other and grey morning light seeped into the hut. Still they did not speak. Both of them knew that words would neither comfort them nor change things. At sunrise he rose and left her as quietly as he had come. Even then she knew that a long time would pass until she would see him again.

*

Summer sleepily passed by. It did not take long until Mairi realised that she was with child. The morning sickness that drove her out of her hut at dawn and the pain in her breasts were clearer signs than the absence of her blood flow. She was equally perplexed and happy. Part of her greeted this new life wholeheartedly, but she asked herself how she could raise a child on her own on this secluded patch of earth. There were hours when she painfully missed the keepers who could have provided her with the kind of support that only women can give to each other.

Her supplies still found their way to the island and awaited her at the jetty each morning, carefully sown into oilcloth, but her child's father she never saw. Sometimes she thought she saw his curragh glide by in the distance, and then she would send a silent greeting over the waters. Her belly began to grow and she found it increasingly hard to use her fish spear quickly enough or to keep balance in her narrow curragh. Once she could no longer go fishing or hunting, she began to find, now and then, some fish or a piece of game between the other bundles on the jetty. And she knew that her beloved watched over her.

*

A new winter made its advent with snow and frost. Winter solstice came and went with its fires and songs and the laughter that echoed over the lake all the way to the isle of swans. As the days grew longer and Brighid's festival of thaw drew closer, Mairi heard a soft laughter sounding in the hidden part of her mind. It was full of anticipation and fell into a thousand pieces hanging in the air from silvery threads. The next day, she went into labour. Mairi fought for long hours on her bed like her mother had done before her. When finally her newborn daughter's cry filled the hut and Mairi's head rolled to the side in exhaustion, she caught a glimpse of a white form hovering in the doorframe. A thin veil, a mother-of-pearl wing gently stroking the wood. Then, again, the pale winter sun. Mairi blinked the sweat from her eyes and then sat up with an effort to take her daughter into her arms. As she breastfed the tiny girl, completely drawn in by her intense gaze, Mairi knew what she would have to do when spring came.

*

She built a new shrine on a small island not far from the isle of swans. There, framed by willows dipping their branches into the lake, the stony fireplace waited for Mairi to light the flame. But Mairi finished it with round white pebbles and slowly extended her own dwelling. She built a bigger cottage from wood and stones that she brought from the mainland in her curragh. Her little daughter, meanwhile, lay on a blanket in the grass and played with her toes. It did not take long until Mairi's slowly progressing endeavours got about to the clansfolk. Some of the men steered their boats to the isle of swans to offer her their help with their usual cautiousness, and she happily accepted it.

*

Summer again, and Mairi abandoned her self-chosen solitude and rowed more often to the mainland to visit the other women. She especially sought the company of the clan's healer and midwife to let her examine the little girl. It was from her that Mairi learned that Sencha had left the lake.

'A bonny healthy girl,' the older woman said and approvingly held up Mairi's daughter. Then she regarded the young woman. 'She's got her father's eyes. Did you know that Sencha, son of Ailill, has travelled east? They say he has gone to bring back his songs to the kings and clans who live under the strangers' heel. There are no bards there anymore, they say. I only hope he will be cautious and take care of himself. That boy has never listened to other people's laws. A quiet rebel, him. It is them that attract the strongest bile. And stay alive the longest.' She smiled at Mairi conspiratorially. 'I fear your little girl here will be a right mule, with parents like that.'

As she rowed back to her island, Mairi pensively watched the child at her feet, who was completely immersed in sucking her fists. 'Your father has gone to sing of Brighid, little Sian,' she said. 'It is just as well that you don't know anything yet of the hatred in people. Because then you would lie awake every night from now on, fearing that he will never come back.'

That evening she sat on the jetty and looked at the newly built re-treat and the shrine that shone white through the willows at the op-posite island's shore.

'Lady,' she prayed, 'I have not forgotten my promise and have not gone to his cottage to live with him as his wife, but I beg you, Lady, protect my beloved from the soldiers and guide him safely on each road that leads him further away from me.'

She knew he had gone to set her free. Maybe he, too, had heard

Brighid's laughter when their daughter had been born and maybe he knew, as she knew, that something had begun then, calling them both and assigning to them tasks whose meaning and pattern they could not yet see.

*

Little Sian grew and thrived, and still Mairi waited for Brighid to instruct her so she could light the flame. And then, one evening in late summer, the women arrived. They were weary and gaunt and told a surprised Mairi of the swan that had led the way, flying afore them, all the distance from the coast. One of them had lost husband and son to a storm on the ocean; the other had been trapped on her way to the market by soldiers who had raped and beaten her.

Both had left their clan's dwellings where everything reminded them of what they had endured. One evening they had followed a strange call that reached all the way into their dreams and would not be silenced. Mairi welcomed them to Brighid's shrine after their long and desperate journey, as once old Sian had done. As long as summer lasted, women found their way to the lake and were brought to the isle of swans by the shy and kind clan folk.

The youngest girl was a child of five years who had witnessed her parents being slain because they had not been able to pay the tenure for their small patch of soil. The oldest was a crone who had seen her son hanged from the barn's gable because he had tried to protect his pregnant wife from the intruders. Each of them, without exception, could tell a tale of random cruelty. Nearly all of them had lost their family and been left behind. Mairi listened to each of their stories and spent the last evenings of the passing summer sitting still on the jetty, her daughter next to her, and was glad the peace in her heart and the love for Sian and her child's father would not allow the bitterness to settle again in her soul as a permanent lodger.

She was shaken by what she learned, and there were days when a powerless rage took possession of her. Something in her cried for revenge for all that women and girls had been forced to see and live through, herself included; revenge for the terror that had destroyed and corroded every sense of trust. It was a demon that would never completely yield. But whenever she grounded herself, became quiet and looked out over the lake's smooth surface where swans glided soundlessly by, peace came back to her. She knew that if there was a place where these wounds could be mended, then it had to be here.

She did her best to help her sisters settle into their new life; she hunted and fished with them, planted herbs and vegetables, built a well and put the finishing touches to the retreat. The lake did one more thing: the rising mists every morning took away some of the spectres disrupting the new keepers' sleep. Slowly the women began, like Mairi, to follow the lake's rhythms. Mairi understood why Brighid had chosen this place to forge the abused castaways of Éire into a new sisterhood. Mairi sang again songs of Brighid, and when the growing band of keepers sat in front of the retreat listening to Mairi's harp the sound of little Sian's gurgling laughter seemed to echo their renewed belief in life and companionship.

When autumn was well advanced and the trees were reflected red and golden in the water, the last keeper found her way to the shrine. Mairi lit the fire and held the first wake. Together with Mairi's daughter, their number was nineteen. Regularly Mairi brought the tiny girl to the shrine on the nineteenth night, the youngest keeper's wake, and sat guarding the flame while Sian peacefully slumbered.

Mairi saw the years pass by as her daughter grew into a bright, albeit dreamy, child who was the very image of her father and had inherited her parents' talent for words and music. The retreat on the lake was well known in the area by now and people came in growing numbers to celebrate the festival of thaw. The nameless island on which Mairi had built the shrine was called 'isle of the flame' by the visitors and at night one could see the light of Brighid's fire shining through the willows, reaching out across the waters.

*

More years passed and the tidings of the isle of the flame brought more and yet more visitors to the secluded place where Brighid's name had survived. They came across the waters to pray in the shrine and took its peace home in their hearts. They listened to Mairi playing the harp and, as time went by, to Sian's singing. Sometimes a visitor told of a wanderer roaming Eíre in secret, telling of Brighid everywhere he found shelter and audience, always on the run from the soldiers. Then Mairi would pause, thanking Brighid and allowing herself a moment of longing.

*

As the retreat anticipated its tenth winter, one of the clansmen in his curragh brought a young girl with a shy but winning smile. When Mairi stepped out on the jetty to greet the newcomer, she felt she was looking through a veil of time into the eyes of another girl to whom she had bidden farewell long ago on the very same spot. Bridie's daughter respectfully took the older woman's hand and bowed her head. Mairi embraced her warmly and accepted the greetings and blessings her old friend had sent her, together with her plea to take on her eldest daughter as a keeper of the flame. Mairi could hear once more Bridie's carefree, cheerful voice, as it had been when they had both been girls, echoing in the young guest's breathless account of home and family.

After Mairi had assured herself that her friend had found her own peace in the life she had chosen, she asked the girl, 'It is truly your wish to be a keeper, child?'

'Oh yes. It has been so since my mother started to tell me stories about when she was a girl and served at the shrine.' She smiled up to Mairi confidingly. 'She has given me your name,' she said.

Mairi looked at her namesake and was equally touched and humbled. She took the girl's hand. 'Come on then, Mairi. I think I know someone who will be very pleased to have somebody her own age to play with.'

Bridie's daughter stayed and took the wake of one of the oldest keepers who had grown too frail to spend nights in the shrine. When this elder finally embarked on her last journey, little Mairi became part of the sisterhood. Soon she and Sian were inseparable and when the elder Mairi watched the two unlikely friends, the quiet and the candid girl, she knew that the single, lost strand of her life that she had brought to the lake had become part of a web again, a braiding of wondrous patterns that had been tied in secret. They were patterns and ornaments telling many different stories: that of the shrine and its ancient flame, that of old Sian and of Bridie, of her mother and grandfather and her clan at the edge of the ocean, that of herself and of Sencha, her beloved. Again and again, a tale of survival, of life in death. Not yet tear-proof, maybe, not without loose ends and threadbare patches, but with substance and meaning and woven by the hopes of many.

Mairi measured time by her daughter, who resembled her father more and more each year that passed. It had been a long time since she had last had news of him. It was the only pain that had remained with her and, though the years had faded the memory of his tall figure and the earnest, enquiring eyes, he came to her in her dreams at night, and in daytime in Sian's slow pensive smile and her considerate way of talking.

When one of the keepers brought the news of his return, Mairi first believed it to be a mistake and thought they must be speaking about another man. But the next day, from her jetty on the isle of swans, she saw a curragh landing on the isle of the flame and made out the figure of a tall man speaking with her daughter in the front yard of the shrine.

Days went by during which she walked as if deep in sleep. She did something she had not done for a long time: she squatted at the shore and regarded her reflection in the water, reached to the fine creases around her eyes and searched for traces of grey in her hair. She wondered whether Sian knew that her father had come to seek her out. She yearned. She waited. But she did not steer her curragh to the lakeshore.

The season was summer and the nights were long and promising. Twice Mairi rowed her curragh to the isle of the flame to keep her wake. Twice she sat by the fire and listened to a maiden's laughter, barely audible, whispering in the willow trees. She did not know how to complete this tapestry of her life, where to tie the last thread. And always in the mornings she returned to the retreat on the isle of swans.

The third night, Sian stood at the entrance of the shrine, waiting for her, as Mairi dragged the curragh on to the shore. A long while they stood there and looked at each other. The young woman wordlessly rested a hand on her mother's cheek. They did not speak, only held each other's gaze, until Mairi's body slowly retreated from the tension and vigilance of the weeks past. From the shore, laughter and the wistful sound of a flute trailed over the water. Out there the young people celebrated the gift of summer. The flames of their fires danced in the night, countless little echoes of the flame kept within the shrine. And Mairi made her choice.

She embraced Sian, Brighid's youngest keeper, who had kept her first wake in the shrine before she had started to walk and who had never thought about a life other than this. Sian who had understood and who had come to set her free. Sian who would gather the loose threads and weave her very own patterns and who would tell her own truth about Brighid.

As Mairi's curragh glided through the smooth water, she turned back one last time. The isle of the flame lay in darkness. But through the trees glinted the shrine's white stones and from its centre a warm glow radiated, casting pools of light on the water in front of her. For a moment Mairi thought she saw a flash of silver amidst the liquid gold, a lithe maidenly form on the shore, a swift movement in the shadows like a stroke of wings, the reflection of fire on white skin.

But when she looked again all she saw was a swan serenely floating on the water, cleaning its feathers. She wondered whether this was Brighid's farewell to her or merely Sian, come down to the shore to watch her mother leave. But as Mairi turned away and steered her curragh towards the shore she knew that there was no difference.

Burning Bride

The Lady on the Grey

Björssi lived on a farmstead some distance from the city. From his window he could look out on to a fjord the ocean had cut deeply into the land. In his whole life Björssi had only been to the city once, when his mother had been admitted to the hospital in which she finally died. Ever since that time he had given any townsfolk a wide berth. They puzzled him. It was as if they spoke a language he could not understand, just as they seemed to little understand him, though the words they used were surely the same.

There was only one big city on the island where Björssi lived, and only two kinds of people. There were city dwellers and there were those who could only be unhappy in the city. That was because the steep mountains, the ice and the fire – the two elements that shared the island in equal measure like an ill-matched couple who had learned to get along over the years – were too deeply etched into their beings to allow them a separate existence.

Björssi's life was the billowing meadows on which his sheep and strong little horses grazed. It was the glacier whose ice gleamed green, red or blue in the quickly changing weather, and the tiny house with its roof made of corrugated iron, snuggled closely to the mountainside. And it was the sea, day in, day out surging on the black sands in front of his window.

He had been born into this life, and during his youth he had sometimes thought of going away, to rent somewhere else, maybe on the mainland or even in the city. But then one September his father and brother had been lost in a snowstorm and never returned from their excursion into the highlands to drive home the sheep. So he had stayed. Now Björssi was neither young nor particularly old but he had been alone far too long on his farm, for the thought of the unknown beyond his home pasture filled him with a vague unease.

He was fond of his rituals was Björssi. On Friday afternoons he saddled one of his horses or took out his father's decrepit van. He stopped at the filling station next to the small general store where he bought his own supplies and some fodder for the animals. Sometimes he stayed on for a cup of strong coffee and listened to all the great and small debacles that defined his neighbours' daily life, and sometimes his own: calving cows, unruly horses, the increasing cost of fodder and the declining fish prices, the girls that fell pregnant far too soon, the young men who drank too much and worked too little, and again and again the hopeless who left their farms or their endless days in the fish factories to try their luck in the city.

Then he would drive home with his purchases through a landscape of bizarre stone pillars and black sands, begotten aeons ago by the fire-spitting mountains that waited on the horizon for their hour of return.

Björssi's one concession to the changes that kept tearing at the edges of his jealously guarded life was the newspaper. It was all about fishing quotas sold to the highest bidder and leaving more than one neighbour without work. It was about increasing the production volume and agricultural cooperatives that formed to produce bigger quantities of meat and dairy products at lower prices. There were foreigners, shipped in from the other end of the world, slaving away for famine wages in the fish factories. And there were the small peasants like Björssi who could hardly remember when their farms had last made any profit to skim a layer off the pile of debts after the fodder and the petrol for the machines had been paid for.

And then there were the village tycoons and factory owners who often had a whole hamlet of tributaries at their disposal. Theirs were the fishing quotas for herring, mackerel and cod, the giant cold stores and the trawlers haunting the coast. For the hamlet people it often meant a choice either to work for those few rich or not to work at all.

The part of Björssi that had been used to hard labour for as long as he could remember was struggling to understand why suddenly this should not be enough. Surely there had to be a way to pay for the few things he needed, to preserve his narrow world as it was. The part of him that grasped the change did not know what to do, and so he left everything as it was. Björssi was a quiet man and the years of seclusion had added to his reluctance to share any of his worries.

There was not much that could cause him unrest, so tightly was he woven into the land in which the elements fought a never-ending battle with each other, and unbound elemental forces were always followed by a curiously forgiving sense of harmony.

No, neither the blizzards and storm surges nor the volcano's mighty tremor, deeply hidden beneath the glaciers, could unsettle Björssi. What could was the notion that he might be forced to leave it all behind. The thought hung in biting icicles from his fears.

Behind this thought lurked an abyss that he chose not to look into. In these moments, Björssi, who had never prayed to any god, called upon the only spirits he knew: the invisible inhabitants of rocks, stones and streams, of the treeless plains and the ocean. And he would have found it hard even to believe in those had it not been for the girl.

He would see her from his window. She rode a wind-coloured mare as grey as the rain falling in spring, she herself as pale as the sea that caressed the horse's hooves. Her ashen hair was tousled by the wind and her swift ride and blown into her face in long, sleek strands. It was a face Björssi had never seen, because whenever he had set eyes on her she had turned her back on him. She would speed along the strand, away from him, until she vanished behind a rock.

When he had first encountered her, he had been no more than a child playing on the beach with pebbles and shells. He had not heard her coming, for she never made any noise. Only a light breeze had made him turn his head just as horse and woman chased along the edge of the sea. He had seen the mare's proud back and the strangely colourless silhouette of her rider, and he had jumped up and run, following her, chasing her, run faster and faster, but she always seemed to be the same distance away. All his pleading calls went unheeded: the mare vanished as soundlessly as she had appeared, and when the boy had wanted to follow the hoof prints he had found the sand untouched.

There were times when he would see her more frequently. In the summer that followed his father's and brother's deaths she had waited for him every day at the hem of the fjord, where he would find her delicate outline and the mare's curved neck set against the never-setting sun. Every evening he looked out for her, and when finally he saw her he would wait silently by his window, since the vain foot races of his boyhood had taught him she would never wait for him nor could he ever catch up with her. Instead he witnessed her wild hunt along the deserted beach, and it left him with a notion about how it must be to be entirely merged into the elemental dance, into wind, surf and rock.

Sometimes he ran out on the beach, threw himself on the sand and made a burrow, deeper and deeper yet, until he couldn't breathe anymore and inhaled the echo of volcanoes, long gone cold, and mighty ice floes that had once ripped apart the cliffs and driven the fjord into the rock.

He recognised the same grinding forces raging within himself, a primordial act of creation, forever destroying and reinventing itself. It was like a gladiatorial dream: the combat of giants unleashed, at last sung to rest by the grim, unchanging rhythm of the ocean.

And in the calm that followed the storm, when the stricken earth breathed heavily, the rideress appeared, danced effortless and feathery through the waves, carrying with her a soothing coolness that smelled of rain and delicate sea foam.

During that summer Björn had learned to respect the fjord for its own sake. He loved it for its vitality, wildness and aloofness and for the simple gift of feeding his cattle, his horses and his sheep. It was nothing he ever talked about – he wasn't much of a talker anyway. Had anyone asked him, Björn could not have described it with words, but that was what he felt and, though he did not realise it, the reason why he felt awkward and stripped bare whenever he left his farm.

The language Björn wanted to know was so old that it could forgo words, forged in the heart of the black earth and the ocean before any human had stepped on the island's shore. It was the language the mountains spoke to each other and the wind to the waves, and sometimes Björn thought that if only he knew the right word the Lady on the Grey would stop for him.

*

In the language of humans, meanwhile, the newspapers reported that the retail prices for milk and meat were dropping further. Bjössi stood by his window, perplexed, looked out on the sea and did not know what to do. He watched his horses playing with their foals on the meadow below. They were good, strong-limbed creatures with graceful movements, and their foals promised to turn into good riding horses. Until now, Bjössi had only trained his own riding stock. The rest of the foals he sold to his neighbours or trusted them to sell them for him, since his cattle and sheep meant enough work for just one man.

It was spring and the days were starting to draw out longer, Bjössi said to himself, and if he used the long bright evenings, the summer that never saw the sun setting, maybe he could train the horses himself and sell them for a good price? It was the only option he could think of. So Bjössi set to work. He mowed grass and baled in his hay. He milked the cows and tended to his sheep. In the evenings he would ride. He took the young ones to the right and left of his experienced gelding to make them feel less intimidated by his presence and his voice. He carefully placed saddles on their backs and, step by step, got them used to carrying his weight. He blew into their widened nostrils to give them a sense of trust. The midnight sun saw him riding over the sand, time and time again, until he returned to his farm exhausted, only to be on his feet again in the small hours of the morning, courtesy of strong coffee and desperation.

One late evening in high summer his legs hurt so much that he had to pull the reins and dismount. With clenched teeth he leaned on a rock that marked the far end of the fjord, and rubbed his knotted muscles. From the corner of his eyes he caught a fleeting movement. The evening sun clouded his sight, and all he could see was a shadow flying by at the rim of his ken. His gelding pricked up his ears and gave off a soft sound of greeting. The young stallion at his side pranced nervously and craned his neck. A pair of warm nostrils blew gently into Bjössi's neck. When Bjössi turned, he looked into the eyes of a dainty grey mare that briskly nodded her head and rubbed her mouth on his gelding's.

The girl on her back pushed a wet strand of hair out of her face and smiled at Bjössi shyly. She gave off a faint scent of the salty foam that hung in her clothes. Björssi was lost for words. 'Well,' was all he could come up with. The girl was still smiling.

'Forgive me, farmer, if I have startled you,' she said. 'Your neighbour, of the Steep Slope, sends me. He said you could maybe do with some help with the horses. Or on the farm.'

Björssi cleared his throat and rubbed his forehead while he tried desperately not to stare at her. The farm called Steep Slope was at the other end of the fjord. Björssi was on good terms with the farmer, Rani, and his family, although he mostly declined the well-meaning invitations of the farmer's wife. He dreaded Rani's mouthy herd of children, his teenage daughters leading the way, forever giggling behind his back.

Rani must have noticed Björssi's solitary excursions along the beach. Probably he, the lone wolf and bachelor, had ascended to be the area's new child of sorrow. He could not quite decide whether he should feel angry or embarrassed. One thing, however, he was more than certain of. The thought of a young woman on his farm drove beads of sweat on to his forehead.

The young woman in question was still standing before him, eyeing him expectantly. It did not escape Björssi how bright her eyes were in her narrow face. They had the colour of mist, sprinkled with tiny chippings of green ice. Minuscule beads of water hung from her eyelashes. Now he *was* staring at her. Abruptly he averted his gaze.

'I don't need anybody,' he said curtly. 'Tell Rani I appreciate his offer, but I don't know how you could possibly be of help to me.'

Her eyes changed then. Into her candid gaze crept something he could not read.

Confused, he threw the reins back over his gelding's head and mounted. 'No hard feelings, lass. I'm sure you know your horsemanship.' He indicated with his chin her gracious mare. 'But I wouldn't know how to pay you, anyway.'

She nodded, still bearing that peculiar expression, then smiled again. Björssi did not look back, but he knew she was still on the same spot, holding her mare's reins, watching him. The young stallion at his side was restless. He wildly tossed his head and kicked while Björssi's gelding flattened his ears and struggled against the bridle. With a determined jerk the young stallion pulled free and dashed off, mane flying, back to the ledge where the girl still was. Reaching her, he dug his hooves in the ground, stopped abruptly and rubbed his head on her chest. Bjössi's gelding jumped and snorted. It took Bjössi a few minutes till he managed to calm his horse enough to ride back to her.

The young stallion was standing contently on three legs and letting her fondle his ears. When Bjössi arrived, she wordlessly handed over the reins.

Bjössi knitted his brow. 'One could be tempted to think you were a mermaid,' he half-heartedly tried to joke. 'Have you come from the sea to enchant my horses?'

She did not answer, but steadily held his gaze. There were spectres drifting in her eyes like clouds the colour of seaweed. Bjössi was feeling uneasy. He nodded one last time. She leaned over and blew gently into his stallion's nostrils. Then she leaned back and released him. Bjössi sped off with the two animals as if the devil's wild hunt was on his heels. Reaching his farmstead, he turned and looked back. The sands lay empty under the midnight sun.

*

When Bjössi entered his stables the next morning the cows had been milked and the sheep had been driven out. Between his horses on the meadow a beautiful grey mare stood and grazed peacefully. Bjössi had not thought it possible he could lose his temper like he did then. Angrily he pushed back the door leading to the horse stables, where the young woman was raking in bales of hay for the horses in training. Unperturbed, she hardly looked up from her work.

'I want you to leave,' he said without ceremony.

She looked at him, and there it was again, that feeling of unreality. Her hair was hidden under a scarf, and her face seemed to be made of eyes alone. Her gaze washed over him like water. He drew a deep breath.

'Why do you want to send me away?' she asked calmly while she fluffed up the hay. 'You are in need of help and I do not want any payment. I live with Rani and have my livelihood. I can handle your animals; you have seen that much.'

'I want nobody loitering on my farm.' The words broke out of him before he could think better of them.

She nodded and smiled. 'Then you are lucky. I am nobody. I come from nowhere and I belong to no one. Now I am here and you need a hand. Don't be unreasonable, farmer.' Her smile was slow and serious and, in spite of her confident way of talking, still rather shy.

'What do you mean, you belong to nobody? I bet you are from the city. Are you a friend of Rani's girls?'

A shake of the head.

'Are you related to him?'

More head-shaking.

'To his wife?'

No reply.

'Where are you from … ?'

'Don't ask so many questions,' she said, and her smile turned a little sly. 'The work will not be done any quicker.'

Björssi rubbed his forehead and regarded her, baffled. One more moment and he would be adrift in her eyes of mist, boneless and unconscious like a creature of the deep sea.

'But you have a name, do you?'

'Sjó. My name is Sjó.'

That night Björssi did not ride under the midnight sun. Instead he watched his new companion trotting up and down the beach on her mare, a young horse tied to each side, never tiring. He asked himself which wave had washed this girl from the deep. This creature with saltwater tangling her hair and with eyes like mist who was called by the name of the ocean: Sjó – the sea.

*

Sjó of the eyes like mist was a good worker. In the mornings she was up before Björssi, regardless how early he rose. And late in the evenings he often had to call her in from the window, so that she brought the horses in for the night and sat with him in the narrow kitchen where they drank Björssi's strong coffee and ate what they could conjure from his supplies. In the beginning they hardly talked.

Björsi was embarrassed. Under her intense gaze he always felt as if his contours were dissolving while soft showers rippled down his back like warm rain.

'Don't stare in your cup like that, farmer,' she would sometimes mock him. 'Rather look there – the sun is nearly sleeping on the sands.' And, truly, the warm glowing ball of the midnight sun would seem to roll westwards through the glittering surf. The sky seemed to run together with the earth, the fjord with the mountains and yesterday with tomorrow. Time dissolved and what remained was a single, long, hope-filled summer day, in which everything was possible. The ocean had heard him and had sent him Sjó. During this summer Björsi did not read the newspaper.

Sjó ignored most of Björsi's reluctant questions about her origin, her family and her plans for the future, and so he gave up trying to fathom her this way. As the summer turned towards autumn such matters ceased to mean anything to him anyway. Sjó had silently and seamlessly merged into his life so that, slowly, slowly, he began to lose his shyness. It turned out that neither of them was a friend of unnecessary chatter, and so their conversation was mostly confined to the daily work and the training of the horses. At sunset he would see her ride off on her grey mare, and, lying in his bed, he would let the day's images pass through his mind. How her long fingers had combed straw from her hair or how she whispered sweet, unknown words to her fosterlings, leaving them wide-eyed, nostrils flaring with wonder. The closer she was to the beach, the more liquid and smooth were her movements, and with them those of the horses she rode. Her tall silhouette flowed like quicksilver around the horses' eager forms.

One evening she did not ride away, but slept in the small chamber behind the kitchen, and Björsi listened dozily to her soft breaths through the door she had left ajar.

'Well, Björsi? How do you get on with your new help?' asked Rani on one of his short visits that had become even rarer this summer. Björsi shrugged, and Rani grinned roguishly.

'She is able,' said Björsi. 'And she is the best horsewoman that I have ever seen.'

'Not that you have seen many,' Rani teased. 'You've hardly ever left this fjord.'

'True enough,' said Bjössi. 'But there is no need to have seen many to spot an exceptional one. The horses will tell you, and they're never wrong.'

Rani laughed and raised his glass of clear schnapps to his neighbour. 'Wise words, farmer, and I tell you one thing: your horses will be sold at a good price. Here's to that little minx's health, whoever she may be.'

They both raised their glasses, drank a toast to Sjó, whose long shadow floated between the surf and the black sand, hardly visible against the sun.

'So you don't know where she came from either?' Bjössi asked, trying not to sound too curious.

Rani shook his head. 'No. Stood there in front of my door one evening in spring and asked me for work. Wet like a seal, in these oversized clothes, the little grey beauty next to her. I keep asking myself if she has something to answer for somewhere, you know, whether she did anything wrong. But I suppose we would have heard if she had.' He shrugged. 'I guess she has run away from her parents, or maybe her bloke. She isn't a city girl, that's for sure. Not working like that, she isn't.' Rani yawned and did not wait for Bjössi to reply, but bid him farewell and made his way home.

For a while Bjössi pondered Rani's suspicion, but deep within himself he knew there was no living creature on this island who was able to bind Sjó or to whom she truly belonged. He knew that, wherever she had come from, she was as free as only one could be who understood the language of the mountains and the ocean.

*

As the summer withdrew and shades of rust and brown started to colour the fjord, Bjössi sold his horses for a good price and settled some of his debts. The meadow below the house was suddenly deserted. Only Sjó's grey mare ran there with Bjössi's gelding. At first, nothing seemed to have changed: the girl still looked after Bjössi's animals and kept the house in order – and set to repairing the ramshackle iron roof as strong winds started to whip over the farm beneath the mountain. The days ran away and soon the air smelled of snow.

When Sjó finally left, it happened with the same suddenness that had escorted her arrival. They had been out riding together. Usually they did not venture all the way to the fjord's end, but headed back after they'd reached a steep rock that pointed like a needle to the sky. It was the same rock where Bjössi had first encountered his companion. But this time Sjó's mare left the landmark far behind, leading Bjössi's horse on to the far end of the fjord, where the mountains met the sea. Here Bjössi's world ended and only a steep path wound up to the pass that led out of the valley.

The girl reined back her grey and looked at Bjössi with her fathomless eyes of mist. 'Here our ways must part.' She smiled, but her features betrayed neither regret nor hope.

Bjössi regarded her, surprised at first, then helpless, and a convulsive sense of loss took root in his heart. Never before had he felt like that, not when his father and brother had gone missing and not when his mother had passed away. Not even when he had been forced to think about selling his farm. This, this was different. It was as if Sjó was about to take the best part of him away with her, the part that had listened to the glaciers and the ocean, and so to leave him bereaved, naked, without language and expression in a wasteland.

So he said nothing and just looked at her. What was there to say in the restrained language of people, of the city and the newspapers? A language that meant nothing to Sjó. A language in which he himself was held captive, a discordance that once upon a time had held some meaning. Once, once, he had belonged to a song of praise that had long since faded away.

And Sjó of the eyes like mist? She sounded and vibrated so that he could never stop listening to her. And now she would go back, would become once again one with the song that was calling her – he could already hear it in the wind and the crash of the waves. No, Bjössi did not speak, because he did not know the word. His tortured mind struggled for something that could hold her back, make her stay. If only he knew the word. But he didn't, and he spoke not, and into the eyes like mist crept, very softly, a familiar expression.

She waited for a while, and then she lightly touched the cheek of the man who had remained wordless.

'I wish you well, farmer,' she said. 'And abundance on your house. And, farmer … if you ever happen to see me again, call me by my name.' With these words, she turned her grey mare and rode up the winding path. The waves licked at the rock with a strange desperation, as if even they wanted to lure her back.

*

Björsi returned to his farm and to his old life, and when Rani asked what had become of Sjó he only shrugged. Rani cast him long, in-quisitive glances but did not ask more. He only slapped Björsi's back sympathetically. 'Sorry for you, old chap. I thought, you know, it had all yielded up well. For the two of you, I mean. A woman in the house and all that. She seemed happy enough to me, after all.' He sighed, then winked. 'What can you say? Women! I, for my part, have too many of them.'

Björsi only nodded, not really paying attention. He was glad that Rani knew him well enough not to expect any answer.

Two years came and went, in which Björsi sold horses and made his rough-and-ready livelihood. After Sjó left him, he understood for the first time what it meant to be lonely. It was not the well-acquainted loneliness of the hermit which had often caused the neighbouring farmers to shake their heads behind his back. It had never particularly bothered him to not belong to Rani's world – a world in which one would meet up every Friday night at the petrol station, drink cheap liquor and exchange long-expired kinky stories. But now that Sjó had gone, something in him was emptier than before.

This new loneliness was full of sharp contrasting features like the now deserted beach, deep black before the whites and ice-blues of winter. He was banished from the magnificent song he seemed to constantly hear in a far corner of his mind and in which he never could join. He had no room for the longing that called for him in his dreams. There was nothing, nothing but the forbidden chamber in his soul that Sjó had settled in and now had abandoned. Water and wind alone told him of Sjó. The indefinable yearning of old now had the delicate contours of her face.

*

Feeling like that, Björssi finally left his farm. He sold his animals and settled his debts. What little land remained he assigned to Rani. 'I'd rather you have it than a stranger,' he said. 'At least then the fjord remains as it is.'

'I'm sorry to see you leave, neighbour,' Rani said. 'I wish the little mermaid had stayed. Maybe everything would have turned out differently. She had a lucky hand with animals, that one. And with the land. Made them shine, if you may say so. Well, what the hell! It is like it is, eh? I wish you luck. You are welcome anytime, you know that. I will keep your land for you.'

*

When Björssi first woke up to the noises of the city he asked himself whether the fjord would be a little bit emptier without him. Did he belong to it as it was inseparably part of him? Did the black sand remember the sound of his footsteps? Did the silent mountains keep a wake for him? Did the wind swirl around his house looking for him? Did the waves run on to the sands a little higher in hope they might reach him? He almost wished it was so. Maybe that would have been comfort enough to impede the paralysing rigor that spread through the room, crawling clumsily, like slowly cooling lava.

Björssi worked on the docks, and when he was not at work he drank. He wasn't the only one and he wasn't the heaviest drinker, but maybe he was the most unhappy of them. In the numb hours of alcohol-induced haze he returned to a beach, seamed by bold rocks, where he raced against a lady on a grey, whose ashen hair smelled of salt. When he sobered, the paralysing rigor claimed him again. He didn't pray, nor did he quarrel. He never tried to change his situation. He never cried and he never raged, because that did not lie in his nature. He waited.

*

And then, on a cold winter's morning, Bjössi was home once more. From one moment to another he stood at his kitchen window and looked out to the frozen sands, on which the rideress glided by through the sleet, soundless, and vanished into the mist.

Somebody jostled against him. An angry voice indicated that he stood in the way. The promenade by the sea was full of thickly hooded people, buttoned up tightly, hurrying towards their destinations. Bjössi had stopped in the middle of this stream, frozen in spite of the hot flash that had hit him. There, at the edge of the sea, he had seen a pair of liquid grey eyes that had melted the rigor in his soul. He saw ashen hair, falling over a slender back, for a blink of an eye saw her tall figure concealed by a heavy fur cloak, then she had vanished into the crowd. He ran then, pushed his way sideways through the masses of people, tripped, ignored the angry shouts, apologised, and craned his neck desperately to catch a glimpse of her, not to lose her again.

And there she was, dainty, grave, long fingers randomly tracing the cold iron railing, as if she was lost in thought. He ran faster, but the more he laboured, the more distant she seemed to become. He could hear his own panting while he hastened, slipped on the wet concrete, fell down, came back on his feet with effort. He had been drinking the night before and he felt dizzy. Fumbling, he tried to grasp the railing to steady himself, and pinched his eyes against the sudden sunlight. The winter sun reached through the mists, and for a moment water and sky fell together and formed a veil of streaked cold grey. He could not see clearly. He felt her presence vanish. His attempts to call out for her were muffled by the dry sob that rose in his chest and took his breath away. What he uttered was coarse and inarticulate.

And then the veil tore apart. A wild brawl washed over him, the surf clawing angrily at the concrete ripped off the lava-cold rigor, and from far beyond the bay the mountains growled their consent. The wind sang a word to him, now wild and unruly, now tender and fragile, without beginning or end, an echo of eternity that resounded and never had been lost. And this time he joined in, allowed his own voice to be the leading note, until Sjó stood by his side, leaning her cold forehead against his.

*

They returned to the fjord. When they made love Bjössi felt as though their heated bodies travelled effortlessly to the sea's edge, where at last they merged and nothing ever had any meaning except the same, endless rhythm of the tides. And so it was … at least for Sjó, who remained strangely untouched by everything that happened outside her own sphere.

Her persistence and serenity, always the same, had their source in something that also touched Bjössi, and together they gave themselves to it and trusted, since what else was there to do?

They became a mother and a father, and their daughters wove their own tales, thoughts and insights into those of the fjord. Sometimes Bjössi would look at his children playing on the beach like he had done, and his heart would sink. It was the only thing that let him think anxiously about the future. How could he secure a place for them as they grew older? And how to shield them from a desperation that had nearly destroyed him? He watched them playing on the shore, quicksilver swift and as effortlessly aligning with the elements as their mother, and he hoped they would be strong enough. That he hardly saw anything of himself in them did not trouble him much. Whenever he said so, Sjó only smiled.

'You are too humble, my farmer,' she said. 'If they weren't yours also, they would not love this place enough to stay. And who would keep it alive for all that is to come?'

He held her close to him then, and did not ask what she meant, since a part of him knew that the end of their story had not yet been told. Maybe one day he would understand, one day – and a faraway day he hoped it to be – when it would be completed.

They had their own truth, Bjössi and Sjó with her eyes like mist, and many might quietly snigger about them, but everybody could see that the farmer in the house beneath the mountain was a happy man. Everybody could see that he knew how to make much of little, as they say, and for that they had to pay him respect, reluctantly at first, and then more and more sincerely. The horses he sold were the fastest, steadiest and most footsure that could be found in this part of the island, and horsemen brought their young foals so Bjössi's wife would teach them to carry a rider. Bjössi saw his growing daughters fly across the sands like their mother, equally gifted, and equally ageless.

*

As the years went by, Bjössi discovered more and more signs of his own age. Sjó remained unaltered. Her long ashen hair didn't turn grey, her gauzy skin was not wrinkled by the sharp winds, and her lithe body did not look a day older than those of her grown-up daughters. Only her eyes like mist were maybe a trace darker, more tired, and mirrored the many years that had passed. No, Sjós girlishness did not fade, but sometimes Bjössi found her strangely otherworldly and colourless, nearly translucent. He could feel a strange, disembodied restlessness reach for her that sneaked up from the shore and got caught in the seagull's mew. Bjössi watched her when she was riding and the waves seemed to attempt a playful contest with her. They danced and beckoned and through the fjord sounded an ancient calling that every day anew ascended from the deep and rode with the surf on to the sand, where it was scattered among the foam and died.

With every day that passed, that calling became more urgent. It was as if, faced with the ocean's voice, everything else fell silent and the mighty brawl that had given Bjössi his voice again, back in another lifetime, had found its way into the fjord. Bjössi heard it, and felt it resounding in his body. And then, one midsummer's evening, he saw a pearl grey mare dashing riderless across the beach and shaking her salt-crusted mane. That night he made love to Sjó, held her and breathed in her scent that rippled over him like rain and made him feel drunk, leaving an aftertaste of warm, heavy, wet sand. Her hands lay feathery around his shoulders, and the inexhaustible grey of her eyes took away the fear of what was to come.

*

The next day she was gone. He found her clothes on the beach, but no footprints betrayed the path she had taken. The black sand was smooth and untouched. Finally he found the prints of petite hooves where a single rock pointed towards the sky like a needle. They led him to the sea, where he followed them along the water's edge until at last they vanished, swept away by the sea that bore a familiar shade of grey.

Lorelei

Worse
even than your maddening song,
your silence
Sylvia Plath

Elisa enjoyed telling the story of how she met Christian, because it was unusual. The more predictable her life became, the more she held on to the extraordinary. It was Elisa's graduation day. She stood on deck in her smart suit and heels, appropriately forlorn and melancholy, while the cruiser carried her away from the pier. The venerable baroque façade of Bonn University, presiding over the river, slid out of sight and charged the situation with suitable symbolism. Elisa had tried to feel regret, but was only mildly stirred by the melancholy of the scene.

Had she had access to money, or one of the scholarships that were given to those who were able to afford the elite schools of the country, she would not have chosen Bonn, or Germany for that matter. She sometimes wondered where she would have chosen. Not Florence or Paris – too obvious – and not London – too vibrantly eccentric – or Berlin – equally avant-garde, and shabby besides. She would have liked Venice, she thought. It had the right balance of glamour and morbidity.

Elisa had often pictured herself in a spacious flat above one of those narrow cobblestone alleys, looking out on to a canal. She imagined it would have been a feast to study there, where art seemed more real, not neatly stacked away in the rotunda of the Academic Collection of Arts in Bonn.

Sometimes the days she had spent there, surrounded by gods and goddesses on their pedestals, drawing the curves of haunches, buttocks and gracefully arched backs, had made her skin prickle. Standing on the deck, she felt a surge of longing and thought she would have liked that time to continue. Then she remembered her tiny bed-sit above a Turkish sweet shop and the cheap booze parties in the museum cellar, and she thought better of it.

Sometimes she had gone to luxury boutiques and let her fingers glide over silks and satins until they tingled and ached for more. When her parents had asked her what she would like to do for her graduation day she had said she did not care, they should decide. Then she had thought of Caspar David Friedrich's paintings, and Lord Byron's fierce praise of the Rhine, and in her mind has risen the image of steep cliffs, of dark, shady woods and ivy-covered castles. Her parents had been delighted with the idea of a boat cruise. Thus Elisa stood on the deck in her smart suit and heels. Hers was a well-staged exit. She congratulated herself on having done all she could. Considering.

*

Christian's father had just died and Christian had stepped out of the house and walked the streets like a stranger, away from his mother, from the body on the bed, from the doctor who had come to record the death. He had walked over Adenauer Bridge and stared for a long while at the boats gliding by. He thought about how he had lived in this town all his life, a town patronised by the stately silver band of the river – Father Rhine, they had called it in the old days – and never gone for a cruise.

As he queued to pay for his ticket Christian found himself staring at a young woman who stood in the line before him among the chatting members of what appeared to be her family. Her dreamy gaze was directed at the river. She looked ordinary enough, but she radiated an absentness that separated her from the noisy, ice-cream-indulgent crowd. She wore a straw hat that she held secure with one hand while the other clasped the handbag that had slid from her shoulder, pulling her linen dress so he could see tanned flesh that made his groin twitch. He was suddenly curious, a strange sensation when mingled with the pain and confusion that had ruled in his heart just moments before.

As the boat steered towards the middle of the river, Christian felt the summer in his blood. The elusive girl sat at the other end of the boat and looked up at the castles with their shadowy towers, enthroned high over the Rhine like reliable but grumpy guards. The banter of her lively relatives was a strong antonym to her self-absorbed haziness.

Later, Christian wondered whether he could have sensed what was to come. But the only thing he saw there and then was mystery. The day his father died, the day he went out on the river, Christian lost his innocence. It had nothing to do with the limpidness of a boy outgrowing childhood, or the discomfort of adolescence. It was the taste of obsession.

Over the mountains the sun began to set, and the river glowed in shades of rose and purple. Christian felt a strange anticipation. It was the kind of twilight described in fairy tales. The hero or heroine found themself lost in ancient forests where they encountered unicorns and speaking animals. Anything seemed possible.

*

When Elisa laid eyes on Christian sitting by the railing she thought she had never seen anyone so openly vulnerable. Somehow, with his boyish features and mobile face, he seemed larger than life. She had been reminded of a statue she had once seen in a museum in Rome. It was a boy who pulled out a thorn from his foot, frowning, his whole form set to the task of removing the source of pain. That marble boy had been so present in the moment – every chiselled fibre of his body, his curly hair falling into his face, and his brow knitted with concentration. It had been mundane yet supreme. And it had caught her attention. Not much did in those days.

Christian was beautiful in a way mothers thought their sons were beautiful. He had something pristine about him. What she liked about him most, Elisa found, was his head. There was a Greek god waiting to come out. His mouth was wide and reminded her of the sultry youths in Botticelli's paintings. She wanted to kiss it.

Her observing eye could also see that he was in pain. Elisa had studied enough twisted bodies and tense faces to recognise the imprint of agony. She regarded the strain that had crystallised in the young man's features. She thought it was rather interesting.

The boat trundled sideways and then sheered out, following the wide stream of the Rhine as it snaked around a very high and steep rock reaching out into the river. A shadow fell over Christian's bent head and he looked up at the gloomy cliff under which they passed.

'Have you ever heard of Lorelei?' the fairy girl asked, standing at the railing next to him.

*

Christian smiled at Elisa, and did not know what to say. She repeated her question. 'You must have heard of Lorelei?'

'"Lorelei" as in that legend where she sits on the cliff and sings and all the fishermen die because they stop paying attention to the current?'

She smiled serenely. 'The very one. They say the Rhine is very dangerous here. Many must have died over the ages. Maybe that is where the story comes from. They were looking for an explanation. A tale to tell the children left behind. Something less trite than being smashed on the cliff by the current: "Daddy is never coming back. Daddy was taken by the siren mermaid."'

He looked at her composed face and, for the first time, into her strangely wild eyes. 'Oh,' he said. 'Oh. It's here, right? This rock? This is Lorelei's rock?'

'Yes. It's where they say she sits and combs her hair and sings so sweetly that the fishermen forget everything. They do not look at the waters. They have their gaze on her alone.'

He cleared his throat. 'Scary.'

She shrugged. 'If you believe in it.'

He regarded her, intensely. 'Do you?'

'Oh, please.' Her mouth twitched again and then settled into a half smile.

'But I like the story,' she added. 'I like myth. Or how it is depicted. Did you know that her name is related to the word "lure"?'

Christian silently shook his head. He was still staring at her, hungrily, uninhibitedly. How strange, Elisa thought. You would think he'd have lost that look by now. Have been taught better. Surely, he must be her own age. At least.

'Are you a historian?' he finally asked.

'Art historian.'

'Studied in Bonn?'

She nodded. 'You?'

'I'm an occupational therapist.' He paused. 'I work with children. Really enjoy that.'

'I bet you do.'

They sat for a while in a silence that Christian thought was charged with sex. Elisa always preferred to think it was meaningful.

*

Sometimes, when they made love, Elisa would seize his shoulders and press hard and whisper, 'Stay like that.' And Christian would do as she asked, without questioning. He would have done anything to please her, to soothe that wild look that entered her eyes sometimes. He did not move, but could feel her gaze wander over his body, scrutinising, drinking him in. Absorbing him. At first, it excited him. But after a while he began to feel limp and strangely lifeless. When she asked him to stand naked by the window, with his eyes closed, he refused and fished for the jeans he had thrown on the floor. She was hurt. She said she did not understand. Why did he have to be difficult?

'Sometimes I think you only want to look at me,' he said.

'I don't know what you mean.' There it was again, the pain that made his face so alive. She felt the urge to see more of it.

'Like a painting,' he said.

'And is that a bad thing?'

He shrugged, irritated. 'I don't know.'

Elisa held out a hand to him. Her body, tanned and solid, lured him in where her strange request had repelled him.

'A painting isn't real,' he said.

She looked at him, and he stared back, blankly.

'How do you know?' she asked. 'Maybe it is the only reality there is. All is condensed in art. All is reduced to essence.' She leaned down to caress his chest, and he forgot that he had wanted to escape.

Why do you always stay on the surface, he wanted to ask, but he did not find the words.

*

Christian and Elisa became what their friends began to call a 'never-ending story'. They had split up four times in three years, and made up again. They had slept with other people: Christian to erase the accumulating pain, Elisa because, on rare occasions, she spotted somebody who made her palms prickle as once they had when she was drawing Greek sculpture.

Christian still worked on the ward. He had started to think he would like to have children of his own. Elisa had enrolled on a PhD in classical archaeology, dreaming of a post in Rome or Athens, knowing that it would never happen like that.

Christian was neither naive nor in denial. Over many a pint with his friends he would consent that he should maybe move on and find someone who was less of an 'ice queen', a term that his mother, who could not stand Elisa, frequently applied to her.

But he thought of the giant in a fairy tale he sometimes read to the children, a selfish giant who refused to allow the children to play in his walled garden. This giant suffered terribly when they left for good and eternal winter settled over all his greenery. Christian was still hanging around the garden door, waiting for Elisa to open it and invite him into the icy wilderness.

Whenever he grew tired of it and made preparations to leave, Elisa would kick the gate wide open, a look of terror on her face, and her body suddenly tangible. They would make love then, hungrily, and she would cling to him, whispering she was sorry. He would bury his head in the hollow between her neck and her shoulder.

'You are the end of me,' he said one time. How pathetic that sounded! People in novels said things like that and it usually got them nowhere.

'I can change,' she said. She sounded convinced she could, and knew that she couldn't.

'I love you,' he said. 'But I wish I had never met you.'

Elisa put her hand on his cheek. 'I'm sorry,' she said. And meant it.

They finally got engaged – it was Elisa who asked Christian, though she insisted on keeping her own flat. She needed to have her space, she said. She needed it to work in. Christian gave in and hated himself for it. He would withdraw in an attempt to control his desire, and Elisa would ring and come round to his flat, ready to fuck him into oblivion.

There were times when they did not call each other for days and it was a question of who would give in first. Christian called it their 'phone game'. Once, during one of these intervals, he had a dream. It was a hot August afternoon and he had come home from work and stretched out on his sofa to take a nap. In his dream he drifted alone on the middle of a river. The boat had no oars, and he was vaguely aware of his powerlessness.

The water was quiet, and over the mountains in the west the sun had begun to set. His little vessel danced on the waves like a nutshell. There was a cliff with sharp reefs reaching far into the river. They looked like suitors wading into the water in pursuit of an impossible task, who had been petrified for failing. He wondered who could have done that to him, and then he looked up.

High above him, on a shoulder of rock, sat a woman, beautiful and terrible in her nakedness. Her long pale hair flowed down to her haunches, and her skin was translucent like water. Her dreamy eyes met his for a moment, then drifted away, to a mirror she held in her hand. With the other hand she began to comb her hair with lingering, patient strokes.

'It will become easier once you have died,' she said with Elisa's voice. It sounded almost compassionate. Christian choked in terror.

'I don't want to die,' he cried out, trapped in the boat that had begun to turn and twirl as it approached the reefs.

The woman did not lift her gaze from the mirror. 'I can't help you,' she said. 'You have to go all the way.' And without looking at him she began to sing.

In his dream Christian drowned. As he was sucked under by the angry waters he could see the sun. What broke through the surface from above was an equal share of darkness and light.

*

She had done it the way Christian would have predicted had someone ever asked him in jest, 'If Elisa wanted to kill herself, how would she do it?' He heard it on the news, after having tried to call Elisa for days without getting an answer. She had worn her great-grandmother's bridal gown, all silk and lace; above its high collar he imagined Elisa's face pale and serene, like a fin-de-siècle Ophelia. Her legs and backbone had been broken when she hit the surface of the river after jumping from a ledge in the rock called Lorelei, more than sixty metres above. She must have done it at dusk, for only one cruiser had seen the woman falling fast though the air, before the current took her away.

Christian remembered Elisa talking about the dress: hand-stitched and embroidered with exquisite blossoms and Brussels lace, its former mother-of-pearl glow faded to sepia. He wondered how he could ever have hoped for a wedding.

'There is so little grace left in these times,' Elisa had said when she showed him the exquisite gown.

'Maybe it is you!' he had shouted, exasperated. 'You always want to make life grander than it is.'

Christian grieved, but wasn't sure whether it was Elisa he mourned or his own disenchantment. He missed her terribly and at the same time felt like someone who had had a close escape. His counsellor said resonant things about borderline and narcissistic personality disorder, but Christian knew, in a place in his heart that had fallen silent when Elisa's song stopped, that there was more to it than that. For a while he tried to see the world through her eyes. He only saw shades of grey.

When, years later, Christian visited Lorelei's rock with his own children, he saw the statue for the first time. It sat in the entrance of the harbour opposite the cliff, catching the summer sun on its bronze back. It was a woman with a body made for a goddess and long hair cascading down the length of her back.

'Who is that?' his daughter asked and tugged at his sleeve.

'Lorelei,' Christian replied.

The little girl shook her head impatiently. 'No, it can't be.'

Now she had his attention. He looked down on her keen, up-turned face.

'Why not?' he asked. 'This is how the artist made her. It is what he thought she would look like.'

'But Lorelei is a wicked woman. You told us the story. She made people drown, didn't she? But this one, this one is very sad. See?'

It was true. As Christian regarded the statue's features he noticed the pain etched into them, the agony of the too powerful. In his mind he suddenly found himself beneath the rock, looking up at the cold fay woman of a long-forgotten dream. But what he saw now was not a seductress. 'You have to go all the way,' she had said. He hadn't, in the end. Elisa had.

The Witch of Hollow Hill

> As long as you have a garden, you are alive.
> And as long as you are alive, you have a future.
> *Frances Hodgson Burnett*

Inside the hill above the town there lived a witch, they said. The truth was that she had been hanged up there. Yet truth was not something that greatly occupied most people in town. It was an old folktale, the inevitable ghost to pull out of the closet at Christmas when grandparents became sentimental and wanted a haunting tale to tell. And haunting it was, haunting and sad and everything a story-teller could wish for.

It was the tale of a girl who had been buried in an unmarked grave far from consecrated ground. Nobody knew her name, or whether she had been ugly or fair, blonde or brunette, tall or petite. The only feature the story mentioned was her eyes. They were a witch's eyes, Grandma whispered to the children by the fireside; eyes as green as a splinter of dark ice; knowing eyes, the eyes of a crone in a maiden's face. And so the town had hunted her, for those eyes had scared the wits out of them. They were eyes that had understood the soul of the people. But nobody knew that. It was a secret she had taken to her grave.

*

In the town overlooked by Hollow Hill lived another girl with green eyes, albeit in a safer time, or at least safe from witch-hunting of the kind that had made a ghost of a girl five hundred years ago. Her name was Rhiannon and she was distinctly pretty, distinctly spoiled and rather lost. But she did not know that. It was a secret yet to be revealed to her. She was not particularly fond of nature, since it of-fered her no opportunity to indulge herself. In fact, it was the only arena she knew in which she did not command an outstanding position. So when she came to Hollow Hill to meet her fate Rhiannon set out with an expression of misery. But there is no such thing as coincidence, some say, and no place for vanity in nature.

Rhiannon had been invited for a ride on one of her schoolmates' horses. She went because the grace of her friend's white mare had hooked her the minute she had laid eyes on her. On the mare's back a new meaning of grace unfolded before Rhiannon, who at the time was too occupied with trying not to fall off to fully appreciate it. She followed her friend into the woods leading up to Hollow Hill, dazzled by the exotic sensuality of being carried by such a nimble creature. It was midsummer and the forest was bathed in dappled sunlight.

Rhiannon turned her face upwards, so that tribal patterns of light and shadow were painted on her skin. She felt the sun on her body and she thought, *How exquisite*. She liked all things exquisite but had rarely found them in nature. Then again, she never spent time in nature. She preferred the town, with its shops, cafes and ice cream parlours, where she could be seen and adored. She was addicted to being adored and would have found it hard to remember a time when it had not been part of her routine. At sixteen, she had already learned how to comply with men's fantasies. She had perfected the toss of hair, the crossing of legs and the way her little finger stroked the rim of her glass, as if by accident, when she drank. She knew how to dress. She knew when to speak and not to speak. She knew how to look deep and sensual to make up for a lack of profound things to say. But today she found herself on Hollow Hill, where she last had been as a child. And to her astonishment she was enchanted by it.

'I didn't remember there was a secret garden,' Rhiannon said to her friend.

The other girl stopped her horse and looked at the ivy-covered gate. 'It's where they hunted down the witch. Don't you remember the story?'

Through the bars, Rhiannon caught a glimpse of bluebells and roses. Her own story began to fall back in place.

Nan came to the garden nearly every day. Although the house was deserted and the windows broken, the garden was in a surprisingly good state. Nobody had lived here for twenty years, not since King Henry had ransacked the place and arrested the Squire for not acquiescing to the new truth, this new Church of England that had brought so much death and confusion.

Nan loved the garden. She loved its mystery, its pools afloat with water lilies, its alcoves, the billowing sea of flowers and the arched bowers covered in ivy. She loved the deep scent of summer, and how this secret world rejoiced and indulged in its own beauty, unconcerned with the woes and cares of humans. Ever since she had come here as a little girl, Nan had served the garden. She had weeded the flower beds, cleaned the pools and cut back the ivy. She had cleared the pathways and cut the roses so they would grow more beautiful the summer to come. And so they did: salmon and pink, purple and yellow, they peeped out of every corner the summer Nan turned sixteen and her father told her she was to be married.

Nan's father was the village's blacksmith and a huge bulk of a man. Nan was afraid of him, though she had learned not to show it, for her Pa feasted on fear, and whenever he sensed it he craved more. And now he had decided Nan was to marry Tom, the son of the apothecary.

'You like plants, don't you, Cat Eyes?' he had joked when he told her. It had been one of his better days. On his bad days he called her 'Witch Eyes', much to her mother's distress.

'Hush,' Nan's mother whispered, 'Don't say things like that. You never know who might be listening.'

Her Pa looked at Nan and her slanted green eyes as deep as the woods around Hollow Hill. 'It was you who gave birth to that changeling, mistress. She has this strangeness about her, Cat Eyes has. Lucky enough we found someone wants to marry her. And good with all that grows she is, too. I'm a considerate Pa, I am. Lots of plants and herbs and the like in the apothecary's shop. Aren't you happy, Cat Eyes?'

But Nan wasn't happy. Nan was happy when she was in the garden. And there she went when she had heard the news, to hide in her favourite alcove, for she did not want to marry anyone and certainly not the apothecary's son. He was a scallywag, and he had bad skin. He also groped Nan's breast or backside whenever he encountered her alone somewhere, knowing that Nan's Pa would only laugh and brush it off as boyish awkwardness, should Nan ever dare to tell him. No, Nan could not stand the sight of Tom. The prospect of sharing a bed with him made her feel ill.

But in this year, when Nan turned sixteen, something happened. The boy king, the sickly son of iron-fisted King Henry, died, and his sister inherited the throne. And since she was a Catholic, things changed rapidly in England. So it was that a young squire returned from exile to his rightful abode at Hollow Hill.

*

To Rhiannon's surprise the gate had been unlocked. The two girls explored the garden while the horses peacefully dozed in the shade of an old hawthorn bush by the gate. Rhiannon walked between the flower beds and let the ferns stroke her calves. She pushed up her sunglasses and was hit by a dazzle of colours. A bunch of carnations swayed in the breeze and caressed the sensitive bare skin of her leg and a ripple of pleasure shot along her spine.

'Not bad, hey?' the other girl said.

'Huh?' Rhiannon folded her arms as if to protect her bosom. Suddenly she felt vulnerable in her short tank top exposing most of her midriff. She cast a glance at the white mare dozing contently in the sun. The horse's eyes, with their absurdly long lashes, were half closed.

'That is the most girlish-looking horse I have ever seen,' Rhiannon said.

Her friend shrugged. 'Can't blame her. Has to keep the boys keen, like the rest of us.' The look she bestowed on Rhiannon revealed only a glimmer of jealousy.

'So what about that story then?' Rhiannon asked. 'Is it really wicked? I can't remember it at all.'

'Let's sit down over there, in the sun, shall we?' the other girl said with a yawn. 'I brought a picnic. I suppose if I think hard I might remember how the story goes.'

*

Nan's Pa had shod the new squire's white mare. It had caused Nan to hang around the workshop until her father tripped over a bucket while trying to squeeze past her.

'What is this, you dim-witted wench? Since when are you idling about, being in my way, when all you usually care for is these herbs and buds of yours? Just as well that the Squire is back now. Stops you from prowling where you don't belong.'

Nan had pressed flat against the wall to escape the hot iron he was waving in front of her face.

'It's only I wanted to look at the horse, Pa. Isn't she a fine creature?'

Her father, usually unconcerned about beauty, had a soft spot for horses.

'Aye,' he agreed, grudgingly. 'I suppose she is now. It's a woman's horse, that one is. I can tell.' He cast a look at his work.

'Now, Witch Eyes,' he said. 'While you're here you could as well take her back for me. But don't linger. Those fine folks don't like village wenches creeping about their gardens, do you hear me?'

Nan's face lit up.

'And make sure they pay you,' he called after her, when Nan had already scrambled up the mare's back with the easy grace of youth.

From one of the bowers in the garden of Hollow Hill, the one overlooking the woods and pastures, the young Squire could see a rider on a white mare weaving along the narrow pathways. It was a hot midsummer's day, and in the garden the flowers were in bloom and the bees hummed lazily, like wedding guests taking their time to indulge in the feast spread before them. The young man in the bower shaded his eyes from the sun. Shadows cast by a few scattered clouds played on the green and darkened the shape of a young girl riding his precious mare in a man's fashion and without a saddle.

Now she was approaching the hill, slowly making her way up the winding path through the wood. It was then he called out to her the first time. Whether the trees had swallowed his call, or whether she did not want to hear, he could not say. She disappeared and reappeared between the branches, lost in her own thoughts. Her hair, he saw, was chestnut brown and shone in the sunlight. He called out a second time. And suddenly the sunlit path was empty. Bewildered, the young man leaned over the wall, trying to catch a glimpse of her where she would reappear on the path coming up to the main gate. It remained empty. He called out again. Only the birds answered him. It seemed as if the hill had swallowed maiden and horse. But then, suddenly, from the bottom of the garden, he could hear laughter. It sounded like a rustle of wind in the ferns.

*

They never got round to the story. After eating, they had stared up into the clouds for a while and then dozed off in the sun. Before she slipped into her dream, a thought passed through Rhiannon's mind about the danger of freckles. Her head rolled to one side and before her eyes closed she looked at a particularly prickly thistle displaying one single purple flower. *Thorny bitch*, Rhiannon thought. *What have you got all those prickles for? This garden could surely do with a bit of weeding.*

And then the garden fell away to both sides where an entrance opened at the side of the hill. Rhiannon mounted the white steed waiting for her at the gate.

'Where are we going?' she asked.

'Inside the hill,' the mare answered, her long lashes discreetly cast down. 'You will see.'

They went down for a long time. The path was narrow and winding and led through countless caverns and rocky passages. Roots hung from the ceiling, forming a strange musty counterpart to the green bowers above. The further they went down, the damper it got. The air grew cooler and little rivulets of water ran from the walls. Soon the mare's hooves splashed into pools of water with every step.

'I'm not sure about this,' Rhiannon said.

'Not long now,' answered the mare.

The Squire found Nan sitting by the pool that caught water from the stream flowing down the garden terraces. The mare was grazing by a hawthorn bush nearby and did not seem impressed by the arrival of her master. Nan looked up and saw an agitated young man, slightly plump round the middle, who was trying to catch his breath. He had a kind, delicate face that wore an expression of utter puzzlement. What the young man saw was the Queen of Fairies who had come to entertain herself in his garden. The girl seemed to him like one who had escaped from a masked ball, like someone who could be seen dancing among countless lanterns playing on a moonlit lawn on a midsummer's night. Only she was not dressed up at all; quite the opposite. Her gown and simple cap could not have been more unassuming. But the way she trailed her fingers through the water, her skirt pulled up from her slender calves and bare feet, the suppleness and poise of her body – all made her look like something sprung from a folktale.

She could be a nymph, the Squire thought, *or a dryad, more at home with the flowers, fountains and trees than the world of man.* To him, in that moment when he first looked at Nan, she was the spirit of the garden. She baffled him so much that, on reflex, he bowed to her. The moment he did it he realised how ridiculous he must seem.

Nan bid him good day and cast down her eyes as she had been told to do when faced with nobility. But then she was seized by a fit of giggles. She couldn't help it.

'And how would you have got in here, lass?' the Squire said, trying to sound stern.

More giggles. Surely, Nan thought, she was about to get into trouble.

'Who are you?' asked the Squire. 'What business have you with my horse, may I ask? Are you the blacksmith's lass?'

The thought of her father sobered Nan, if nothing else could. She nodded, her eyes still cast down. The Squire felt a strange urge to see her eyes. As if she had read his thoughts, she lifted up her head. He looked into a narrow, freckled face. Not beautiful, he thought, instinctively, trying to make sense of her. Then he saw her eyes, and a ripple went down his spine and spread to his groin.

What he saw was a perfect mirror of the splendour around him. There seemed to be everything in this garden of her eyes. The young man's heart started to beat violently. He could hardly breathe for this strange sensation, something he recognised as desire, but which felt much more pure, much more truthful. As if the girl's gaze connected him to something deep and important, something that only few would be allowed to see. A whole private world of beauty, complete and content in itself.

'There is a gate, you know,' Nan said. 'You just have to know how to unlock it.'

The young man blinked.

'What?'

'A gate,' Nan repeated patiently. 'At the bottom there. Behind the bluebells and the roses. The lock can be lifted through the bars if you have small hands.'

She held up a pair of slender hands, not too clean. Her mouth twitched into a smile, half shy, half mischievous. He was hardly listening. He wanted to go astray in her eyes.

*

'Look, I'm not sure about this at all, right?' Rhiannon said to the mare. She was vaguely aware she must be dreaming.

Her companion nodded and snorted softly. 'We are nearly there. See?'

Rhiannon stood up in the stirrups and craned her neck to see what 'there' meant and, in the process, realised she wasn't wearing any clothes. Gasping, she slumped back into the saddle and slung her arms around her breasts.

'For God's sake!' she said. 'I want to wake up!'

'All in good time,' the mare replied.

Rhiannon became angry. 'I'm bloody stark naked!'

'I can't see much difference,' said a voice at her side.

Rhiannon jumped and spun round. A girl stood there at the entrance to yet another cavern, half lit by what appeared to be candles. She was smaller than Rhiannon and she had hair the colour of ripe chestnuts. The number of freckles on the girl's face was like one of Rhiannon's personal nightmares. Her eyes were slanted, green and unsettling.

'What do you mean, you can't see much difference?' Rhiannon asked as aloofly as possible.

The girl looked her up and down.

'You was not wearing a lot of clothes before. When you was up in the garden.'

'Look, can I go home please?'

The girl spread out her hands. 'You came here. They all come, one time or other. They come riding down.'

Rhiannon was puzzled.

'Who comes here? Who is "they"?'

The green-eyed girl looked up at her with an impish half-smile. 'The girls,' she whispered, and she giggled softly. 'They want to learn about the garden.'

'What garden? The one at Hollow Hill?'

'All gardens. They are all different, are they not? But they are all the same, in a way.'

'I haven't the faintest idea what you're talking about.'

'Tell me about your garden,' the strange girl said. 'Is it very beautiful? Is the gate open or locked?' She eyed Rhiannon intensely. 'Open, I dare say. Wide open. No wonder it is all thistles.'

'You've lost me already,' Rhiannon said, trying to sound bored.

The girl was unimpressed. 'You want a secret gate, really.'

Exasperated, Rhiannon slid off the horse and stood shivering before the smaller girl. 'What do you mean, a secret gate?'

'You are very beautiful,' the girl replied. 'You could do better than thistles.'

'What are you doing down here, anyway?' Rhiannon looked at the mushy walls and the clusters of roots all over the ceiling.

'I make the garden grow. I make it beautiful. I have no greater pleasure.'

'I can tell. Have you been hanging around here for long?'

'A while,' the girl said, with a dismissive wave of her hand. 'Not hanging, though. That was long ago. They cut me down pretty soon.'

*

It was Tom, the apothecary's son, who found them out. At first he had not known why he was suspicious. But Nan, *his* Nan, as he had come to think of her, had such a glow in her cheeks lately, and if Tom was sure about one thing, it was that it had not been him who put it there. So he had begun to follow her. He had lost her, at first, quick and clever as she was, and his hands were too clumsy to reach through the bars of the gate. But he could hear her laugh in the distance and he hated her for her happiness.

Nan and Martin. Martin and Nan. She loved to hold him around the middle. He was ashamed of his podginess. He tried not to show it, but she knew anyway, and she kept silent.

'Dear heart,' she would say to him. 'What shall we plant for next year?'

'Oh, I know what I should like to plant,' he would say, because he knew it would make her laugh. All the same, she seemed to sober more quickly as the summer passed.

'You know it cannot be,' she said.

'Why not?' he asked, though he knew.

'No one can stay in the garden for ever.'

Theirs was one long, enchanted summer. He would watch her running along the stream, naked.

'You are like Eve on the first day', he joked.

'Before the tree, and the apple, and all that sad business,' she said, her eyes alight.

'Before,' he agreed.

*

'You shocked me there, you know,' Rhiannon said when she had regained some composure.

The girl shrugged.

'I still make the garden grow. It is all I ever wanted. It would have been worse to marry Tom. He would never have allowed me to go back to the garden.'

'Who's Tom?'

'Never you mind, my dear.'

'It could do with a bit of weeding. The garden, I mean.'

The girl cocked her head and flashed her playful smile. 'There is always somebody who finds the gate,' she said. 'Now you have come. You could help. It could teach you a thing or two about flowers and thistles. And locking the gate sometimes. Also, the summer rain would do you good.'

'Please stop!'

'Makes the skin smooth and soft. Especially when you don't like freckles.' The girl narrowed her eyes. 'A bit of a bully, is he?'

Rhiannon, cross-legged on the ground, folded her arms. 'Who?'

'Your Pa.'

'I suppose.'

'Mine was. That would explain why you always think you have to please boys. Men. Why you want to make sure no one can compete with you. It would explain why you let everyone into the garden of your soul. There is a secret place that belongs to you, and you alone. A place of beauty, that needs no tending by anyone but yourself.'

Rhiannon gaped at the elfin girl. 'How dare you, you … you spooky weirdo!'

The girl met her gaze fearlessly. 'I just look closely, that's all.'

'I don't give a fuck, you know.'

'Ah, but you should. I did not. Look where it got me. You want to be careful.'

'I bloody am. I know what I'm doing.'

'Keeping your Pa out but letting everybody else in?'

'I'm not fucking …'

The spirit girl put a finger to her lips. 'There are a lot of Toms out there.'

'Who the hell is Tom?'

'You want to tend the garden above. You will understand.' She smiled. Her small hand stroked Rhiannon's cheek. She gathered up her old-fashioned skirt and was gone. There was a breath of warm air in the small of Rhiannon's back.

'Come on,' the mare said.

Before she mounted, Rhiannon put her arms around the warm neck and rested her head against it.

'I'm cold,' she said. 'I'm cold inside and out.'

'You will not stay cold, dear heart,' the horse said. 'The sun is up there, waiting.'

As they climbed up the steep narrow path a thought came to Rhiannon.

'Are you dead as well?' she asked.

The mare snorted. 'I can't remember. I believe I must be. I have brought many down here.'

'And her? Did you bring her down?'

Rhiannon could feel the mare's back stiffen.

'It was me that stood under that tree with her on my back. They brought me out of the stable. They pushed her up on to my back. Her own father did. They put the rope around her neck.'

There was a pause.

'And she fell.' Rhiannon said softly.

'She slid off my back, just like that. She hardly weighed anything at all.'

They both fell silent.

'What had she done?' Rhiannon whispered finally.

'She believed in beauty,' the mare said. 'They both did.'

As they turned the corner Rhiannon suddenly saw the sunlight.

*

Nan and Martin are bathing in the deepest pool. There is a full moon in the sky and a promise in the air.

'Come away with me,' Martin says.

'And leave the garden?'

'We'll find another one.'

'When the summer is out.'

There is a rustle in the hawthorn bush by the secret gate.

'What was that, Nan?'

'Only the wind, dear heart. It tells me you fret too much.'

'I thought I heard footsteps there.' She puts a finger to his lips and stops him from worrying. She knows how to do it. Knows it very well.

Rhiannon turns her head and looks at the thistle. A bumblebee is feasting on the one single blossom. All the other flowers are still hidden, tightly encapsulated, clinging to the prickly stem. The insect's furry body covers all the colour. Close up, Rhiannon can see it diving into the heart of the flower, indulging and ravaging.

'Not a bad idea, hey?' she says to her friend, rubbing her eyes.

The other girl looks blank.

'The thistle and its flowers,' Rhiannon explains. 'How it only opens one flower to the world at a time. It keeps its secret places.'

Her friend waits for some further explanation. But Rhiannon is crouching in front of the thistle and ignoring her raised eyebrows, so the girl just shrugs. 'Whatever.'

Rhiannon gets up, her legs covered in grass and pollen. 'You know, I quite like it here. I had the strangest of dreams. Something about horses and riding into Hollow Hill. Can't remember a thing, though.'

Her friend regards her, surprised. 'But that's how the story goes. That the hill is hollow inside and a witch lives there. And then there is that bit about her grave under the hawthorn bush, and how her lover left the garden and never came back until he was a very old man, and then he found a maid tending the garden as others had done before her.'

Rhiannon looks around. 'It certainly needs some weeding'.

Her friend nods. 'My mother did it. Gardened here. Before she had me. The women in town organise gardening days to keep up with it. Or so they say.'

Rhiannon smiles and her whole face lights up.

'Well, then,' Rhiannon says. 'I could get used to that riding thing, I guess.' The other girl smiles back.

'It'll give us a tan.'

'Wicked,' Rhiannon says.

As they lead the horses back through the gate, Rhiannon puts her hands through the bars to lock it from the outside. They steal through easily enough.

Nan is alone in the garden when they come for her. Her lover has gone to court and is to return tomorrow. She dreamt away the whole afternoon in her mother's kitchen. It was a hot and broody day, and at nightfall a heavy rain cleared the sky and now the water drips from every leaf and petal, soaking the earth under Nan's bare feet. She slips out of her clothes as has become her habit, and takes a deep breath. The air still smells of rain. Its freshness is intoxicating and exhilarating.

A sweet and heady scent in the air makes her skin prickle. Her hands stroke the petals of bluebells and roses. She bends down and caresses the tiny buds with her lips. A few dewdrops flow down her chin. Aimlessly she wanders through an overgrown bower. Her hands, stretched out, glide over the leaves on both sides of her. She is showered with raindrops like kisses. They fall on her cleavage and flow down between her breasts. Her skin laughs and yearns for more. Her fingers touch the smooth surface of a pool. She wants to drink this wine and fill herself to the brim.

Her hands fold over the centre of her being, the place of source and return. It is alright, it tells her. Everything is alright. Everything is. She is Eve in the first garden. She never led her lover to the tree. He came to find her there.

'You abnormal bitch,' says her father, standing next to the hawthorn bush. His face is red and blotchy. He is angry and drunk.

'You will not see another day,' says Tom. Nan can see that he is aroused.

More and more men spill through the secret gate.

I forgot to lock it. How could I forget? I have been too happy. I have become careless.

As they tie her up she thinks of Martin.

I am sorry. So sorry, my love.

'I could show her how to fuck decently,' Tom says as she stands before him naked and wet and beautiful. 'Before we send her to hell. See who she can fuck there! Maybe the devil himself.' He glares at her. 'Would you like that, little wife-to-be?'

Nan looks at him, looks him straight in the eye. And then she knows why they are going to kill her.

'Ah, but you can't,' she says. 'You can't.' She points to her father. 'Neither can you. Nor any of you. That's why you have to bind me. That's why you have to break me. It's cause you don't know how to love. You kill the beauty in it.'

There is a roar in the air, mingling with distant thunder. Everything happens fast after that. The only thing Nan takes in is the mare. For a moment, she leans her head against the warm neck.

'I'm cold,' she whispers. 'I'm cold inside and out.' There is a breath of warmth in the small of her back.

'Not long now, dear heart,' says the mare. 'There will be sunshine in the garden. The summer is not yet out.'

The Once and Future Queen

The Queen had been wounded and lay dying. Her horses stood idle in the stable, and her maids of honour walked the castle as if enchanted by a deep sleep. Empty were the corridors and deserted was the great hall. Gone were the knights who had gathered around the King's round table. Outside the castle walls no breeze stirred the foliage of the woods.

Few knew the cause of the Queen's ailment, and since she had withdrawn into her tower she had become like an elusive story, something vaguely remembered. None of her subjects had seen her for a long while. The ones who thought they knew whispered to each other in the corridors. They whispered of barrenness, of consumption and of an inner coldness that gave her skin the quality of smooth pebble. But the precious few who understood knew that the Queen was dying of love. She had never born the King an heir, and there were voices that blamed her barrenness for the critical state of the kingdom. But there had been one who never blamed her, and it wasn't the King. There had been one who loved her.

In the Queen's confined world, love had not only opened doors; it had given her a wide sky to embrace from her tower window. She had never known such beauty as love made her see in the smallest of things.

The lover's eye had made a proud and defiant queen humble. She had surrendered for the first time in her life. To truth and beauty, her lover had said, before he began to be consumed by guilt. To sin, said the ones who thought they knew.

He was the King's friend and right hand, and she had always known that it could not last. Now he was gone to seek redemption and had left her without any. The Queen had hoped her husband would abandon her, so she could leave the kingdom, and her crown, and find the woman she had never been except with her lover. Her husband, alas, in his kindness, had done the cruellest thing: he had made her stay. And so the Queen's precious cage had made her pale and wan and she could feel life evaporating from her body into the lazy summer day.

Could she have made him stay? If only she had been more courageous. If only she had found the place where his agony was rooted. If only he had let her touch it. Had she missed the moment to make the right gesture, to find the right words? Had she not smiled enough? Had her skin been too cold after all? Had he, in the end, been repelled by the curve of hips, the wetness of lips, the hidden force of her body? She would never know now.

The Queen's heart was tied up by this torment. She would recall those stolen moments and wish she could have been different. She wished she could have been the woman to make him stay. And then she grew too tired even to wish.

And thus the Queen would have died, had it not been for the crystal mirror in her chamber. Day in, day out, from her bed, she stared into its depths, hardly seeing her own reflection. Day in, day out, she stared, for she was too tired to direct her gaze at anything else. One day, voices began to echo from the walls of the tower in which she lay. Out of the crystal mirror, they spoke softly to her. Through the veil that parts yesterday and tomorrow, myth and history, truth and illusion, her grief brought names to her in an endless flow ... Penelope, Helen, Hipplyte, Sappho ...

They were the names of women left behind, whose beloved had been taken by war, bravado, cruelty or the blinding light of their vision. Through the veil they reached out to this other woman and whispered of kinship ... Delilah, Salome, Ruth, Mary Magdalene ...

As their voices caressed her face, and her bare arms tightly clasped her own body for want of the one pair of arms she wanted, the only arms, the Queen understood ... Gráinne, Rhiannon, Gudrun, Iseult ...

She did not know all the names filling the room and speaking in many tongues she did not understand. It was not words she heard. But she felt them on her skin. They wrapped around her like balm, the sudden presence of something so old it went back to that first spark lighting the darkness of the day when man and woman were driven out of the Garden of Eden. It was the thread that formed an age-old knotwork of courage, of meaning and survival. As that spark of resilience was lit, that spark sleeping in the womb of every woman, the Queen felt the stir of a flame rising. She knew then that love might be a worthy thing to die for, but that it was worthier still to live and to find her place of meaning.

And as she looked into the mirror once again she saw not her own reflection, or those of her shadow sisters, but something else. Far away, somewhere on the border between illusion and truth, rode a solitary knight in search of wholeness. He carried his banner with haughty defiance, and his head was turned away from her, as part of his heart had always been.

The Queen knew then that, whatever she could have done to try to keep him, it would have made no difference. And so, without leaving her chamber, the Queen found the Grail.

There was no Avalon for Guinevere, and no sword in a stone to prove her worth. Although the land wept for her, and the trees hung their heads in grief, and the birds sang a lament for what was lost and could never be found again, the land did not wither. And the Queen did not die.

Ember Womb

The Woman Who Swallowed the Moon

It was a strange business, becoming invisible. Sometimes, when Marta looked at her hands in the sink, they seemed almost transparent. At some point she had given up trying to catch her fleeting image in the shop windows. This was because there wasn't one. It felt like wearing a winter coat inside out: her flesh seemed to have fallen away from her body, exposing all that was soft and warm to the biting cold. Marta did not know quite how to deal with it.

As she did not know anybody else who was becoming invisible, she had no reference. Other people did not wax or wane like the moon. They just were. Marta loved long country walks, kept wellies by the door and had a nice back garden with a pond. She had a job and friends who came round for tea. But for some time now she had felt as if there was less of her every day. She could see herself vanishing. It was a strange business indeed. As she had the choice between telling her employer she was suffering from consumption – quite literally – or going mad, Marta did the obvious thing. She ignored her curious condition.

Each day, Marta grew a little paler and a little thinner, until she looked like rain in a November puddle. There was nothing she could do about it. When her friends came round for a cup of tea they would sometimes pause, puzzled, and look at her.

'Are you quite alright, dear?' the more empathic would ask.

'Of course,' Marta would reply, trying her most cheerful smile. 'Just a lack of sleep lately, that's all.'

And yes, she said, she did eat enough, yes, a little pale perhaps, but she had spent a lot of time indoors lately. The job and all, you know how it is.

The less empathic just narrowed their eyes for a moment and

then let it pass without saying anything. One did not want to impose. People had a right to their privacy, after all.

So Marta continued to become invisible. It came and went in waves, but there was less of her after every seizure. Six months or so into the process, there were large periods of time when she could not see herself in the mirror. She ran from every camera, because she knew her image painfully reflected the frailty of her appearance. She had even stopped going to the swimming pool because her outline had become so blurred, her skin so translucent, that she blended in with the water. So she kept to the refuge of her bathtub.

When the situation was at its most surreal, Marta even considered making her condition public. Sometimes she wondered how it would feel not to care anymore about what people thought, how it would feel to be authentic, even if it meant being an outcast. She tried to picture how it would turn out: the reporters, the camera flashes (that would catch nothing but a blurry shadow), the talk shows and sensation-mongering. And she thought better of it.

Finally Marta had to leave her job because people started to talk. As no one understood the cause of Marta's extreme paleness and transparency, her indistinct appearance and general air of decline, her colleagues suspected drugs or alcohol. There was a consensus that Marta was letting herself go.

Her boss summoned her for a meeting and talked earnestly about responsibility, corporate identity and getting some help. He dismissed her by handing over her notice, neatly typed on company headed paper, along with his best wishes.

*

Marta's friends rarely called on her anymore. The wellies by the door had not been worn for a long time. One starry, frozen midwinter night, she stood on her porch and felt utterly lost. A part of her wished that whatever had taken hold of her would speed up and she would vanish completely, vanish from the pain and the stigma of not belonging. But, alas, there was enough of her left behind to feel the pain. There was nothing to be done, nothing to try to seek relief, and she let herself fall into that agony within; she just wanted to give up.

It was then she turned her face up and saw the moon.

It was full and voluptuous that night, exuding a silver light that seemed to touch her face in greeting. To Marta, it suddenly seemed the most exquisite thing she had ever seen. She felt a strange surge of kinship. That night, a great yearning took hold of her. She wanted to learn the mystery of the moon. She wanted to understand the secret of its waxing and waning and of how it kept the balance between presence and elusiveness. She wanted to make it her own. She wanted to summon it from the sky, wanted to know it intimately and become one with it.

Of course she knew that could never be. It was the moon after all, far away in the sky, but this made no difference to her longing. It was a desire that quickly turned into obsession. Soon the thought of the moon filled Marta's every waking hour. Some time passed and, obsessed with the idea that she had found a remedy for her condition and could not apply it, she fell even deeper into depression. If only she could learn the secret of the moon, her life would make sense again and she would be whole once more.

Another night, at midsummer this time, Marta was watching from her window the reflection of the moon in the pond. It was perfectly round and luminous, as if it had indeed fallen from the sky into the water. And suddenly Marta was struck by an idea.

She fumbled frantically with the door, hands clumsy with excitement, and ran out into the garden. The ground seemed to drown the sound of her footsteps. It was as if the whole world had stopped to witness the completion of her desire. She stumbled over her empty plant pots and abandoned gardening tools – and fell. So urgent was her need, so impatient was she to get to the pond, that she did not bother to get up. Instead she crawled to the edge of the water on her hands and knees with the mindless urgency of the addicted. When she reached the pond, she slumped down on her belly and started drinking.

She slurped and she gulped, she scoffed and she coughed, and she did not pause until the water level had sunk and the pond was nearly empty. And then she bent down even deeper and started to scoop up the water, drinking it as fast as she could from the hollow of her hands. When the pond was an empty dark hole in the earth,

Marta fell on her back, exhausted.

Water was streaming from her eyes, her nostrils, her ears and every opening of her body. Her belly was so full it was close to bursting and she could hardly breathe. Her sight was so blurred by the water that she could not make out anything but shadows at first. But when her vision finally cleared, and her breathing became steadier, Marta looked up to the sky.

The starry canopy above her was unchanged, but the full, reassuring round of moon had gone. Marta waited for the anticipated bliss to come and settle in her body. But nothing happened. She had swallowed the moon, had drunk a whole pond to make it hers, but it had failed to reveal its mystery to her. Instead, she felt ill and even lonelier than before. When she could muster the strength, she slowly scrambled to her feet and dragged her body, still heavy with water, back into the house.

It seemed like the end of all her hopes. But often when you think you have tried everything, when you are at the end of your resources and you finally give up searching, something unexpected happens. And so it was with Marta.

*

At first, she plunged back into misery and her thoughts that night were too black to be coherent. She woke up to a change of weather; the lead grey sky outside seemed to reflect her mood of impending doom. The newspaper that landed on her doormat that morning was spreading panic. The moon had disappeared from the sky, and scientists were predicting all variety of global crises. On the radio Marta listened to several bishops and other religious authorities talking about the Apocalypse. Her neighbours walked past the house looking up to the sky with anxious expressions.

Although it did not exactly make her feel good that she was responsible for the disappearance of the moon, it *did* strangely comfort her. At least this meant she had made an impact – and a rather impressive one at that. And if she could still influence things, surely that meant she was still here, still a human being, still connected with the world of the living, even though people could hardly see her.

This little spark of consolation grew when, some time later, Marta realised her body was waxing where before it had been waning.

As the months of her pregnancy passed, Marta became more and more solid again. Being with child had put an end to her condition, and after some time had gone by without any more vanishing and becoming insubstantial, Marta gained confidence again. She even started to enjoy it. Her belly grew, and she looked at herself in the mirror sideways, smiling. When her pregnancy had become obvious to the outside world, Marta rang up some of her closest friends of old and took her belly round to theirs for a cuppa. It was not hard to find a tale to tell, since in these new circumstances she was not a singular case.

When the time came, Marta gave birth to a tiny but radiant girl child. As she held the baby closely to her and felt the tiny mouth sucking at her breast, she felt a love she had never thought she was capable of. The little girl left all of Marta's friends open-mouthed with adoration. They did not ask how it had come about that Marta, who was not particularly remarkable, had given birth to a child who looked as if she was made of moonlight. That was what they thought, and Marta did not begrudge them, because she felt the same.

Whenever she looked into her daughter's wide eyes, overflowing with gentleness, she knew that she could never be invisible again. She admired the delicate beauty and otherworldliness of her moonchild, but she also saw her own features reflected in the little girl's face.

As little Luna grew, so did her beauty. She had the most loving and generous nature Marta had ever seen in a child. Everyone who was touched by it loved Luna for it. Marta's house became a place of friendship and togetherness again, and Luna filled it with laughter, magic and play. And with her daughter's happy spirit Marta was transformed as well. At times, though, she felt that Luna, however much her daughter, was no more than a guest in her home, a precious favour that Marta would have to return one day. This peculiar feeling became stronger the older Luna grew and the more Marta came into her own as a mother and as a woman.

When Luna was twelve years old, and Marta was the most content she had ever been, the girl started to show signs of restlessness. Sometimes, at night, she would stand on the porch and look up at the sky, a frown on her shiny little forehead. As time passed, Marta would find her more and more often in the garden, looking at the stars as if she was trying to understand a secret she had been excluded from. One night, Luna crept downstairs and stood on the lawn with outstretched arms, bewildered by the silver light that was pouring out of her every pore and illuminating the whole garden.

It was then that Marta, who had seen the girl from her bedroom window, flung herself on to the bed and wept, because she knew the time had come to return her gift. But at the break of dawn she wiped away her tears and went downstairs to give her daughter all the love she had in her heart.

And then, one drunken, lazy midsummer night, Marta watched her daughter walk into the garden once more. There Luna stood, thin and lithe in her white nightgown, looking a little lost. Marta stood by her bedroom window and watched, but she did not move. She did not move when Luna walked down to the garden pond, halting at first, and then with confidence. She did not move when her daughter pulled the thin shift over her head and the garden was bathed in a dazzle of silver. Marta did not move when Luna stepped into the black water, and did not move when it closed over her pale hair, abruptly drowning all light.

And then the light was there again, as radiant and gentle as before, but now it was coming from above. When Marta looked up, she saw the moon again in the sky, an exquisitely carved sickle, ready to grow at its own pace. And this time she did not cry. All around her, windows were flung open and cries of delight and relief echoed through the town. Marta waited for the pain to wash over her and to settle in her bereft body. But the grief did not come. Marta knew that she had completed the cycle. She had gone from waxing to waning and beyond, and at last she had understood.

*

Sometimes Marta still goes out on the porch to look up at the moon, though she makes sure it is not too often. Whenever she does she smiles to herself and thinks of the woman who had wanted to be part of the moon's mystery. But she never lingers. She has learned that whatever is calling from above is only a mirror of what is truly the best in us. And she knows it can never be taken away.

Oshun's Tears

Of the women dedicated to the goddess Oshun they say that
their walk flows like the Great River.

Proverb from Nigeria

When she walked she swayed like the high grass growing on the desert's edge. Her back was long and lithe like a reed and her laughter
pearled softly like water drops from the shepherds' mouths when
they gathered around the waterhole at eventide. When she danced,
her body glided soundlessly like the tiny streams of water that found
their way through the sand in the rainy season. Her arms and legs
glistened like the polished bronze mirror that she wore at her hip,
for Oshun was beautiful, and she knew it.

When she passed the herds on her way from the waterhole to the
village, always a vessel on her head, the men would forget about the
animals. They leaned on their staffs and greeted the woman in whose
footprints was mirrored the beauty of heaven, as the more poetic
among them would say. The quieter ones said nothing, but looked
longingly after her from beneath heavy lids. Many wished to just
once be invited to place their hands on those hips, whose solid
roundness promised them rest after the red hot heat of the day. Oh,
how they longed to kiss those lips, full and tasty like a piece of sun-
ripened fruit. Oh and how they liked watching her backside, that
moved rhythmically to the sound of the sbantu, the long seed-filled
calabashes they took from their bags and played against their thighs
whenever they made out her figure between the scattered animals.
Then her deep laughter would ring across the burning sand, and the
shepherds' hearts would beat a little faster. But none of the men approached her or tried to win her favour with gifts, for Oshun belonged to Shangó, and she loved him well.

Many a man in the village thought to himself that it was a shame
she was not Shangó's first wife, for Oshun was not only fair but also

wise. Her spirit was free of airs and graces, and when she looked at her reflection in the mirror she did so out of gratefulness to the gods who had given her such a glorious body, and such deep wise eyes, in which her husband wanted to drown every time he looked at her. Shangó was one of the village's most respected men. He was young, strong and called a large herd his own. He had three wives, Oba, Oya and Oshun, and many children that made his hearth a happy, cheerful place. Among his women he loved Oshun before all others, for she was closest to his heart. Oya, the youngest, and mother to most of his offspring, had a quick temper but a warm heart and a free spirit. She loved Oshun like a sister and often one could see them sitting together laughing about Shangó's little habits. Had it not been for Oba, Shangó's hearth would have known nothing but laughter and contentment. Shangó worked hard and none of his wives and children had suffered from hunger, though in some years the rainy season came late and the men had a hard time finding enough sustenance for the herds.

But in Shangós house Oba reigned, for she was the first wife. And Oba hated Oshun. Her jealousy made Oba so ill she could hardly sleep at night and would toss and turn on her mat of reeds. When Shangó woke up and asked Oba what ailed her, she only turned to face the wall and would not answer.

Many a night Oba wailed and moaned, and many a night her husband tried to find out what caused her distress. Finally Oba began to cry and covered her face with her skirt.

'It is this other woman, husband,' she sobbed. 'The other, whom you love better than me and little Oya. The fair one, with almond eyes and lips dripping with milk. Oshun, who has only borne two children to you and who you care for more than anyone else.'

Shangó was taken by surprise and completely at a loss. 'But dear Oba,' he said, 'I do not understand. You are the first woman of the household, and you lack nothing. You have beads for your neck and anklets for your feet, you have clothes and finery, you do not go hungry and your children treat you with respect. Both your sister wives respect and honour you. What more do you wish for? Have I ever treated you ill? Have I ever touched you other than in a loving way? I prided myself in thinking that my hearth did not know this kind of women's scorn.'

Oba's lips trembled and still tears were running down her cheeks. 'No, you do not understand! For what do you know of a woman's heart? I wish you had never brought the fair one to this hearth. Before she came you shared my mat much more often. Now you have become a rare guest, so frequently you lie with Oshun! Have you not noticed how vain and full of herself she is? She is forever looking at this mirror of hers, and often I have seen her admiring her own reflection in the waterhole. She deserves neither your love nor that of her children, for she does not love anything beside herself and her own beauty.'

Shangó now began to lose his usually steadfast patience. He angrily replied, 'Your words are full of poison and malice, and I won't have either in my house. There is nothing worse than a hearth where women are enemies, for women are the heart and soul of a house. What you say about your sister Oshun is vicious. I will tell you one thing, Oba: if you do not want to lose my respect, you are best advised not to deny it to your sisters.

Oba howled like a deserted kid goat. 'Your respect! Your respect! It is your love I want, Shangó. The love you owe me and that you save for Oshun alone!'

Shangó rose from his bed and cast a last, cold glance in Oba's direction. 'Oba, Oba,' he said, shaking his head. 'I owe you something, you say? But how can I lie with a woman whose heart is so bitter? My own would wither before the sun rose. What rainy season would bring it back to life?'

With these words, Shangó left Oba, and the night was filled with her keening, which mingled with the distant cries of the jackal and rang far and wide through the desert.

No word was spoken at Shangó's hearth about the argument. Everything seemed to follow its usual routine. Oba held her head high and adorned herself with the most exquisite beads and fabrics. With young and feisty Oya she was friendly and patient and forgave the young woman's occasional clumsiness. To Oshun, however, she did not speak a word. She saved the best pieces of food for her own and Oya's children while Oshun and her two small sons had to make do with second best. Shangó, who was often busy trading at the

nearby markets or driving his herds to a new waterhole, did not notice any of these changes. And Oshun? She kept silent and bore
Oba's humiliations with serenity. It was still her whom Shangó first
sought out when he came home weary from his day. Oba saw herself
more and more an outsider. Even her own children felt intimidated
by their mother's aloofness and bossy attitude and feared her abruptly changing moods.

The more she realised that her behaviour had no effect on
Oshun, the more irritable Oba became. Her fits of temper, only
reined in with effort when Shangó was around, approached like the
dreaded desert storms that could suffocate life within seconds under
a whirling mass of sand. Her hatred burned hot and dry as the air
over the waterhole. Weeks and months went by and Oba concealed
her jealousy less and less. She shouted encouragement to the shepherds when she saw them casting secret glances in Oshun's direction. When the women gathered at the waterhole she laughed loudly
about Oshun's alleged clumsiness and riled the other women with
waspish remarks about Oshun's beauty.

Was it not unfair how her husband favoured Oshun? Was it not
obvious how little Oshun's sons resembled Shangó? Oba's and
Oya's children were the spit and image of their father, but Oshun's
boys with their long limbs and high cheekbones looked so much like
their mother. And was it not shameful how Oshun moved her hips
when walking home over the pastures? There was hardly a man who
did not dream about having her on his mat. Was it not her fault, displaying her beauty like that, so husbands would forget their duties to
their wives? Thus Oba sowed her poisonous seed among the village
women, and they started wondering.

It was true, if they looked closely, that their husbands cast longing
glances after fair Oshun. And jealousy took root in their hearts. When
the women took their vessels to the waterhole, they regarded their
reflected faces, turned and twisted themselves to observe their bodies
and their finery, and many a wife went home to her hearth in a state
of dejection, dwelling upon all the flaws she believed she had found.
Many women now raised their chin haughtily upon encountering
Oshun, and did not greet her. Some even hissed a quiet curse behind
her back. Oba, observing all of this, could often be seen with a smile

of self-contentment, and Shangó, not suspecting where this new equilibrium sprang from, even sought again the intimacy of her mat.

It was the time of the yearly drought, the time before the rainy season once more brought relief for men and animals. In the village at the desert's edge a mood of despondency prevailed. Heat heaved itself over the roofs and brooded above the cracked soil of the gathering place. The air flickered and mirages hovered over the sand. Some of the shepherds, usually accustomed to the sun's puzzling game, lost their way and came home exhausted and irritable long after sunset. At the oasis the water level fell day by day and the people began to save drinking water. Irascibility and impatience settled upon every hearth. Children squatted thirstily in the shadows and their parents tried to save their strength where they could. In the withered steppe the animals roared with thirst and died under the torrid midday sun. The villagers waited for the rain so they could breathe again. But the rain did not come.

First came helplessness; then fear. What had they done to spark the gods' scorn? The people gathered in the middle of the village and sang the rain down to earth until their mouths were so dry they could not force out a sound. The sorcerer clad himself in skins and danced his juju until he fell down unconscious. But the rain would not come. At Shangó's hearth Oba's eyes relentlessly followed Oshun, who gave her own water rations to her children and who, though she was as exhausted as everyone else, looked as blossoming and beautiful as before. It was as if the drought could not harm her body. Her skin was unchanged and velvety, her eyes shone and her face did not wither and shrink like the other women's.

When the rain had been overdue many days, Oba stepped into the gathering place and called upon the village women. The men watched her silently from the shadow of the baobab trees. But there was neither scolding nor disagreement. When all women were gathered, Oba did but one thing. She raised her hand and pointed silently towards Oshun, who stood in their midst, tired, with sagging shoulders, but blossoming and shapely like a freshly watered seedling. And the women turned as if they had but one body and directed their gaze upon their sister who seemed to embody the whole imbalance of their lives.

115

For a while Oshun stood her ground, straightened her shoulders and pushed out her gracefully curved lower lip. But when the women drew the circle closer around her, this lip began to tremble and she stepped backwards. She withdrew, slowly first, then faster, until she stumbled and fell down. The women froze.

With an effort Oshun raised herself off the ground. Dust had settled on her face and she coughed. Slowly, slowly, she let her hands glide over the sun-baked earth. She spread the yellow clay on her thighs and her breasts until her whole body was covered with it. Vanished was the soft glow of her skin, vanished the soft contours of her body. It was a sexless creature with dull eyes that finally rose and left the village, alone, and walked into the desert.

In the village, Shangó and his children grieved for Oshun. Shangó, who had always prided himself on his ability to judge situations, tossed and turned on his solitary bed at night and asked himself whether the women's trial had really been as unjust as it struck him. Their decision had been supported by such a strong unity that Shangó wondered whether he had not seen the evil that had lurked behind his wife's beauty. But had she not always been his trusted lover, caring for him, placing her hands intuitively in the right places when he came home with sore muscles and weary limbs?

Shangó's heart was tormented with shame and guilt, but what could he have done? It was the tribeswomen's age-old right to hold trial among themselves; to interfere would mean turning the world's order upside down. And if they all were convinced that Oshun had brought nothing but misfortune to the village, they could hardly all be wrong? But Shangó was a man. Though he was gentle-hearted and knowledgeable, little did he know about the depth of hatred that women can hurl towards a woman who is favoured by a man. Now that the women had located the source of evil, said the sorcerer, it would soon rain and everything would be well.

But it did not rain. Not on the day Oshun was made an outcast. Not the day after. Endless days passed by during which death sneaked into the village like a velvet-pawed predator. It struck the elderly first, and then the children. Thirst and weariness took their toll and in Shangó's hut the veil to the realm of the ancestors was worn thin. They could hear them calling and whispering in the shadows. It was one of Oshun's sons who died first. His father found him in the morning, stretched out on his mat of reeds, very still and with empty eyes.

Shangó did not have the strength to sing the keening as befitted the occasion. So he cradled the boy in his arms, wrapped him in colourful blankets and carried him out into the desert. Soon also Oba's and Oya's children became feverish and started hallucinating. Oba tore at her hair and shook with pain and helplessness. She could see life leaving her children's bodies, once so feisty, and their souls slowly reaching out towards the veil separating them from the realm of the ancestors. With eyes rimmed red and beyond herself with grief, Oba looked to Oya, who sat in a corner of the hut, her limbs thin and sharp, her eyes sunken in a face that had long since lost its roundness.

'Go and find Oshun,' Oya whispered. 'Go into the desert and find the outcast. We have done great harm and the gods hate us so much that they call all our children away. Find Oshun. Find Oshun, Oba.'

And Oba rose with much effort and, sobbing, set out to the waterhole, for there, she knew, she would find the outcast – if she was still alive.

At the waterhole, now no more than a foul-smelling puddle, squatted a grotesque creature of sand and yellow clay. Only its brown face gave away that it was of human kind; a face so sad that the ancestors that had come to call her away were weeping behind their veil. But although Oshun had suffered the hardship of these long weeks of thirst, her flesh was still healthy and strong beneath the dirt. The suffering had etched her features and made her beauty, once tender, austere and compelling. The creature at the waterhole was the saddest and the most beautiful the desert had ever seen. And since her body did not ail, it was her soul's torment that yearned and stretched towards the veil and called upon the ancestors through the abyss of time to come and bring relief.

Already she could hear their rhythmic chanting, welcoming her. She could hear a little boy's giggling, so familiar, as if it were her son calling to her. She missed her children so much. They were the only thing that could keep her in this world. But she would never see them again; Oba had seen to that.

117

Oba found Oshun half unconscious beside the polluted water and with her pleading lured her back into the world of the living. 'Your son is dead,' Oba cried, sobbing uncontrollably and clinging to Oshun's soiled feet. 'Please, oh please, come back. Come back with me, before all the children die and no laughter is left in our village.'

Slowly Oshun began to comprehend what Oba was telling her. So this was why she had heard her son laughing from behind the veil. She looked down on Oba, motionless. Between ragged sobs the crouching bundle at her feet uttered the same plea again and again, begging Oshun to undo what she, Oba, had caused in her blindness. Oshun regarded Oba for a long while. And then she began to cry.

She did not cry for her dead son, because she had glimpsed far enough into the world of the ancestors to know that they had welcomed him. Too far had her soul strayed for her to return for good. It was compassion for those she had loved and were still alive that made her tears flow. She cried for Shangó who had lost his son. Her lover who would have to live his life shadowed by the shame he had brought upon himself. She cried for Oya who was hardly grown and who feared for the lives of her children. Oya in whose eyes she had seen doubt and fear as she had been forced to leave the village but who had not been brave enough to raise her voice in her sister's favour. Oshun also cried for Oba whose desperate lament proved that she had finally understood the scope of what she had manifested with her jealousy. Oba who had always made Oshun respect her for her determination and spirit but who had chosen to look only to what she thought she was denied.

Oshun's tears ran down her cheeks and left tracks in her gown of clay. The tears ran down between her breasts and dripped from her belly on to the earth. Oshun had many tears of compassion, and the stream flowing from her eyes seemed endless. More and more drops fell on to the cracked soil around the waterhole and also into it. At first they hissed when they hit the baked ground and evaporated before they could transpire. But slowly, gradually, the earth gave way and took in the water gratefully, to became soft, smooth and cool.

Oshun cried and cried until her tears had washed all the clay from her body and she stood tall in her former magnificence, ample and fertile amidst the dying land. And still she cried, cried and cried, without a sound, and her tears filled the waterhole until she could see her reflection in its clear surface. And still the stream of tears would not cease. What had not fallen from the sky streamed from Oshun's eyes huge and shining like the mirror she had always carried at her hip. Oba raised her head from her arms and stared incredulously at the rivulets that streamed from the other woman's eyes without cease and ran into the waterhole in countless creeks. Already it was close to overflowing. And in the end it did.

The water edged its way through the sand and grew, grew bigger and bigger until it was a brook. Until it was a river carrying clean drinking water. And at its well Oshun sat and cried for everything that was lost and could never be found again. She wept for love and guilt and innocence. Many days and many nights she sat there, and her tears fell steadily. Long since had Oba returned to the village. Long since the people had come running from their huts to scoop up the water with both hands and drink. Long since had they carried out the children to receive the life-giving remedy. Long since Oya had come out, supported by Shangó and the sorcerer, to see the miracle with her own eyes. They stood at a respectful distance, full of wonder, and gave silent thanks for the blessing Oshun had given them.

Soon the river's strong current ran towards the horizon, towards a faraway ocean. It carried yellow water enriched with sand from the desert, but it tasted delicious and plants and animals living near the riverbanks thrived on it. It did not take long before the first children bathed in it and the elders sat in the shadow of the baobab trees growing by the banks. The fertile soil beside the river let seeds grow more quickly than the reluctant earth of the village's former plots. Thus a new prosperity came to the village at the desert's edge. Even in the dry season the water level never fell so much that the people would suffer from thirst. And Oshun? She had at last followed her tears, had dived into the floods to catch up with her soul that had travelled so far ahead. She alone heard the trilling, shrill song of triumph that the ancestors intoned to welcome her. She alone heard her son's chuckling laughter.

Her name, however, remained in the world of the living. It was passed on in the shepherds' songs telling about the many gifts of the river and in the dance of the women who gathered on its banks when the dry season came to an end, to give praise and thanks. Thus Oshun and the River of Tears became one in the minds of the people. Had not her walk been like the gently flowing water, her grace like the rolling waves of the Great Stream?

When the women went to fetch water they looked at their reflections in the surface. They turned and twisted to have a proper look at themselves, to wrap colourful cloths around their hips or to adorn their hair with beads. Some liked what they saw and they carried back their vessels with hips swaying and eyes casting coy glances at the shepherds leaning on their staffs.

There were some who only saw what they considered imperfect; they left the waters in a mood of dejection and could not be helped. Some, though, took some time to find and claim their beauty. And the longer they looked, at their faults and at their loveliness, the more they could see the spark in their eyes, and their reflection seemed to bless them with a smile. And the longer they looked, the more the sparks seemed to jump over and dance on the water, turning it into a wide golden-brown band that glistened like polished bronze.

Many griots and sorcerers travelling the markets on the desert's edge sing the river's praise and tell of its blessings. And many become curious to come and see it with their own eyes or to leave an offering at the wooden shrine built in Oshun's honour. But if you are afraid of your reflection, they say, do not come there. At times it is a mirror.

Mater Dolorosa

Among rusty brown hills and fruitful dales, somewhere in Tuscany, there once lay hidden a grotto with a black Madonna. It was carved into the rock on the rear side of a steep hill, surrounded by peach trees. Some long-forgotten hand had put her there, a hand that had lovingly carved a stern face from darkest ebony wood, and into the severe folds of her gown had cut the foreboding of a grief not yet encountered.

The valley people often visited her. There was never a time of year when the Gothic arch from under which she looked out over the valley was not adorned with gifts and offerings. There lay flowers and fruits, wine in big, bulbous bottles and dried corn dollies and garlands of olive leaves. There was never a time of year when the people in their ochre houses with the lopsided shutters did not go home from the grotto with grace in their hearts. There young maidens sat and plaited love knots – for the Madonna to make their beloved catch their eye at the next dance. There kneeled pregnant women who prayed for a safe delivery, or men whose wives or daughters lay in labour.

And every year, at harvest time, they all came. Pilgrimed up the overgrown path and sang from dry, thirsty throats praise to the dark mother of compassion, before the big feast started on the village green. The seasons came and went, and soon the first peach petals fell on her stern face of ebony, soon the sun's heat bleached the royal blue of her mantle. In autumn the scent of olives filled the valley and was carried up the hillside. In winter a pale moon peeped through the trees' frozen shadows and illuminated the child that sat upright in her lap, looking into the distance – all the way to eternity, or so the women in the village would say.

In the village beneath the hill, with its narrow lanes of cobblestones and the houses of clay and crumbly brick, lived a girl who loved the Madonna well. Often she would run up the path when she was supposed to be at school or her classmates were playing hide and seek in the maize fields. Long hours she would sit there and hold a silent dialogue with the black Madonna's harmonious, eternally indifferent countenance. She told her of her joys and sorrow, sang songs to her she had learned at school and placed sweetmeats in the outstretched palm. And no matter how sad or upset she had climbed the hill, never did she leave it without comfort or some notion of trust. This trust took deep root in her soul, and so it happened that she grew into a woman light-hearted and without suspicion. But then war came to the village on the hill.

One night, alarms howled in the nearby city, and the people gathered on the village green, anxiously looking into the sky. Aeroplanes sped across, swift as arrows, and left fire, death and desolation in their wake. Flames danced high on the horizon and the whistling and bursting of grenades tore the valley's peace and drove the people into their cellars, where they held on to each other, shaking and horrified. Some of them found shelter in the church and lay on their knees in front of the altar, praying to burned-out candles. There, in an alcove, sat a young man and a girl who had hair the colour of wild honey. They held each other's hands and together listened into the darkness. On the street beneath the hill, heavy artillery crawled through the night and made the washed-out, lopsided houses shake in their foundations.

The next day, the young man left the village with many others, wandered through fields laid waste and past ruptured stone walls, to enlist in the big city. Having quietly bid him goodbye and waited until he had vanished from view, the girl hastened alone up to the Madonna's grotto and cried until her tears were all offered to the brittle rock beneath her cheek, waiting for a benediction that never came.

She thought of all the treasured hours of secrets and kisses they had shared by the grotto, thought of how numb and useless her womanhood felt without him and thought of the aeroplanes and the artillery that had stolen the peace from her heart. The Madonna's eyes rested on her twisted frame, waiting patiently, waiting for a comfort she could not give the girl. When dusk painted shadows on to the rocks and the girl clumsily rose and moved her stiff legs, she saw that the Madonna's lap was empty and a big piece was broken off the arch under which she sat.

With a muffled cry she picked up the Christ child's head from under the debris, his eyes huge and full of questions in his destroyed face. As the girl looked up and again met the Madonna's gaze, she saw for the first time the sorrow that lay, sealed and hidden, beneath the composure and kindness. And she knew that the pains in her own heart were as old as mankind and that the agony that follows death and loss had not spared the Mother of God.

'Mater Dolorosa,' she prayed then, 'Mother full of sorrow, where can we be safe, where can we dare to love, if darkness does not pause in front of your grotto?' Many years would pass until she was finally given an answer.

Life in the village became hard now that the men had gone and only the very young and the very old had stayed behind. It was high summer, and the girl with hair like honey, whose name was Giulia, worked long days in the vegetable plots and fruit orchards. She laboured hard, milked her old neighbour's cattle and walked alone the many miles to the next village to trade fruit and vegetables for soft cheese for her grandmother. The shelves in the village store emptied and no decrepit vans came scuttling up the road to bring more supplies. The days were long and hot, the nights heavy from stale heat and from fear.

At night she listened to the detonations, and in the morning she saw the pillars of smoke that gave away the place of destruction. But, as winter drew closer, the shadows of war came creeping across the fields like ugly creatures born of soot and lead grey frost. With winter, hunger came. The summer's supplies were quickly used up and no intelligence about the battle's progress got through to the village. Instead, refugees passed by the hillside where the Madonna looked down with sorrow on the bent shoulders and pointed faces. The Mayor tilted his head too, though not quite so compassionately, and sent them away. Giulia ran up and down the ragged lines and asked after the soldiers. But the hollow-cheeked, exhausted women only shook their heads and hauled themselves onwards.

Life in the village only asked for the next day: the olives were harvested, and with them the last touches of colour vanished from a landscape gone bleak, strewn with sharp-edged ruins. Giulia's visits to the grotto had become rarer and rarer. Cold, hunger and fear of the aeroplanes kept the villagers in their houses. But on Sundays Giulia would wrap herself in her long shawl and trudge through the morning frost up to the grotto. There she would sit and think of her beloved until her legs went numb from the cold. The Madonna sat on her throne of bedrock and sadly looked towards the valley, one hand stretched out in a gesture of benediction, the emptiness in her lap mirroring the barrenness that had stricken the land at her feet. The same barrenness was reflected in the young woman, a crouching, sexless figure who rested her cheek on the cold stone.

*

Many months had passed since Giulia's beloved had left the village, and there was no news of him or the other men. The strangely surreal life amidst the noise of detonating grenades and distant volleys of gunfire had gradually spun them into a cocoon of timelessness in which there was space for neither fear nor pain. Only in the short hours spent by the grotto did Giulia grieve for her beloved whom she had lost before their story had truly begun to be told. Sometimes she prayed and asked the Madonna to watch over him and bring him safely back to her; but he was already so far away, her life so much changed, that she found it hard to imagine a time without war and desolation. Even if she did not leave the grotto with her old lightheartedness, the silent, ageless presence of the Madonna did her good. In the Madonna's grotto, within the winter-cold hills, an unexpected guardian angel grew in the young woman's soul. He was one of endurance, a spirit formed by a kind of boldness that can only spring from deep grief, and he would follow her all the way back down into the valley.

When the first hostile artillery rolled into the village, the foreign soldiers found it abandoned. The villagers had left nothing but empty bedsteads. Their once carefully tended cattle roamed the streets aimlessly, lowing in distress and kicking their swollen udders. Up on the hillside, in a grotto formed of rock, a fading note was hidden behind the Madonna's back, telling where they had gone.

*

The fights went on and the tide would not turn. In the big city, refugees lived among ancient ruins from days of a long-faded prime and the debris of their newly crafted counterparts. Between rubble, dirt and dejection, Giulia fought the exhaustion that made her grandmother lie in her shelter more and more apathetically every day. Each day, refugees died in the streets from hunger. Each day, more came, on the run from the hostile artillery, crouching in doorways and frozen gutters. The hospitals were overcrowded with soldiers and had no space for the fragile and the motherless.

Endless numb days went by in search of scraps to feed on and petitioning unknown soldiers who would regard Giulia dismissively while she stood there and smiled at their smirking before they threw her a can of something or a leftover from their rations. Then she would show them a photograph, usually stored away safely in her pocket, but each of them would just shake his head or pat her shoulder, sheepishly, all of a sudden not knowing where to look. They would become friendlier then and give her blankets, chocolate and woollen stockings for her grandmother.

*

One night Giulia heard once more the unsettling staccato of the guns, which had been quiet for a while, and then the earth began to shake. Tank convoys, rolling into the city the next morning, brought soldiers of Giulia's own country for once. They beamed and blew kisses at the silent crowds of gobsmacked people who were trying to take in the news. When at last they understood the victory, the silent city erupted in cheers. The soldiers leaned down and squeezed the hands of women and waved to the children who skipped alongside the tanks. Among them was Giulia with her crumpled photograph, looking into each face, heart pounding, shouting the same eager question time and time again.

Had they not seen her beloved? Did they not know where he was? In every face she found kindness, pity and, often, the shadow of an equally urgent pain – a wife? daughter? betrothed? – but never the flash of recognition.

The celebrations went on for several days. Fires leaped up high on every square and illuminated hollow but hopeful faces. Giulia wandered the city, never tiring, showed her photograph and studied the soldiers' faces and their disturbingly old eyes. But it was always the wrong eyes; it was never the face that she carried with her in her soul. In the end, one of the countless pairs of eyes held her gaze, and she saw a very young man who slowly reached into his uniform pocket and produced a similarly battered image. It showed two boys who had their arms wrapped around each other, laughing. They had the same frank smile and dark curly heads.

The boy looked at the photograph, plucked at his uniform, a bit lost, and then pointed to the space next to where he sat. He met her gaze again and then, slowly, tentatively, hunched his shoulders. It was the blankness in his face that made Giulia put her arms around him. They grieved together, held a reluctant wake in a world that had turned upside down and blown all bridges behind it. On that night, Giulia buried all hope of ever finding anything more than a faded photograph hidden in her pocket.

She left her hope on the heaps of rubble within the burned-out houses and commended it to a Madonna carved in black ebony who too belonged to another, happier time. Then she followed the young man with the dark curls, so that together with him she could attempt to survive.

*

It took a long time before the marks of war began to fade. Giulia's children played between ruins that were only gradually replaced by houses, squares and parks. The war went on even longer in the hearts of the people. Often Giulia would wake up to her husband's terrified gasps as he wrestled with his demons, their visits as unexpected as Giulia's own. It invoked in her the image of a village under the blazing summer sun and a girl with hair the colour of honey who belonged to a different age and whom she did not wish to meet. Her dreams tricked her, unpredictably disrupting the tidiness of her flat and the neat sophistication of her family life.

She was an attentive wife, was Giulia, and a loving mother, working in a bright office the colour of freshly peeled almonds. Late at night she would look one last time into her children's room to watch them sleeping. When she saw their unruly curls mingling on the pillow, she was filled with relief. The smoking debris belonged to the past. Regardless of her gratefulness, behind the veil of death and ashes lay a village with olive orchards and hidden therein an unforgotten pain. Yet she still believed in her children's laughing faces and the appreciative smile in her husband's eyes. Her life followed a quiet routine, interrupted only by childhood diseases, first days at school and Holy Communion, Christmas holidays and shopping trips to the big city.

It was a composed Giulia who, with her gloves of delicate gauze and her red lips, sat in church next to her husband, polite and mindful, if only a bit dispassionate, because part of her belonged to a village of old and to a grotto beneath peach trees, where bitterness lay in waiting for her. She would always avert her gaze from the Madonna sitting in the side chapel and looking quietly down on her. The only one who had a notion of the dark dread lurking in her nights was her husband, but he never spoke of the ghosts of war. Their silent agreement had barred grief and horror. They had encapsulated these things into well-proportioned dreams whose terror lasted only one night, so their days could belong to life.

Only rarely, when Giulia spent the summer holidays in the country with her children, would the ghosts not go away easily. She stood alone as dusk fell, by the gate of the old farmhouse they were staying in, and saw her beloved walk up the dusty road in his ill-fitting uniform. And then the girl she had been ran, ran against time and death, until the veil of dullness fell again and the old enchantment drifted in the air like an unanswered question.

In these evening hours, Giulia allowed the pain to wash over her in waves and the girl with honey-coloured hair to hasten up to the Madonna's grotto, to rest her cheek against the rock and cry, while the gloved fingers of the woman clung to the gate's wood. It was in one of those moments that she decided to go back one day to the grotto. A long time passed, though, until she finally made the journey.

When her youngest daughter's marriage procession passed

through the city's streets, where many years before heavy artillery and tanks had cracked the cobblestones, Giulia opened the cupboard of her dresser and found a dog-eared cardboard box. It contained some old letters and her grandmother's death notice, a battered photograph that in all the years of her marriage she had never looked at but had also never found it in her heart to throw away. For a long time she held it in her hands and looked at it, then she stored it away in her handbag and walked with her daughter to church. The next day, she took a southbound train to see if she could recover the ghost of the girl she had once been.

Giulia slowly walked through the olive orchards, once so familiar to her, in the direction of the red hills that still patiently watched over the village. As she followed the uneven cobbles up the road, passing ochre-yellow houses from which the plaster crumbled, she realised how similar this village was to the one behind the veil: a clear cast of the hazy image in her memory. Still, these were not the same streets through which the girl she had once been had walked uphill to the black Madonna.

She did not quite know whether she should be relieved or wistful. Now that she had found the boldness to meet her old self, she was suddenly afraid the girl would be here no more; here, where life had moved on the same way it had in the desolate city. She looked up at the walls flooded with sunlight and caught glimpses of tidily scrubbed kitchens and generously filled larders and searched for links to the life that had been torn away from her. The children on the streets stopped shyly in their play, stepped aside for the elegant stranger and followed her with their eyes.

Giulia left her luggage at the village inn and chatted a while with the amiable landlord. Many names passed between them, some illustrated by eager gestures the landlord used to point out a current address, but most of the names once so familiar to Giulia produced only a regretful shrug. When an energetic wind announced the arrival of evening, she set out for the clearing in the peach trees. She climbed the steep path with expansive strides, fingers closed around the photograph in her pocket. Even before she laid eyes on the Madonna's graceful hands raised in benediction, Giulia knew she had achieved her end. At last she had found a place that, unaltered, had kept the memory of her old life, of the girl with hair like honey.

It was here she had sent that girl in the night of the victory pyres, to save the love in her heart before it could split and wither like the grotesque world that had surrounded her. Without thinking, at last without thinking, she knelt before the ebony face that had seen the pain of all the worlds and had kept that love safe in the empty space that once had held her child. Together with the girl she had been, Giulia rested her cheek against the rock and asked for redemption.

This time the pain did not come in the dreaded, nauseous waves, but as an almost peaceful presence, nearly as physical as the dark green leaves of the trees. She invited it to join her silent talk with the Madonna, and it settled next to her like an old companion and gave Giulia back her heart. Slowly darkness fell, dripped through the branches and glided up the rock. The Madonna's tilted head faced her, the ageless smile unaltered, knowing and forgiving. Giulia placed the image of her lost love in the niche behind the statue, to join all the other offerings the villagers had left there telling of their sorrows great and small; telling of their belief in grace. There, breathless from her hasty run uphill, she had hidden a note while the village people waited for her on their carts. Lost was the note, faded first, and then blown away, fallen apart at the Madonna's feet like last year's flower garlands.

For a moment Giulia stood again on the dusty road and saw her beloved vanish behind the olive trees. She let him go again, and this time, wondrously, his love stayed on. Giulia understood. She had tried to cut herself off from the pain's sharpness, had embraced it, fought it and at last resigned, but time had worn away her grief, had washed it in the tides like driftwood. What she now gathered were rare pebbles, gently changed and devoid of sharp edges. These treasures bore the memory of her demons, but they also preserved the best in her: her strength, her tenacity, her loyalty and initiation into the true essence of being human. There was connectedness, there was truth: with her children, her husband at times, with life in the abyss of death. She saw the laughing, carefree face of a girl with hair like honey, and she invited her back in.

Night came, and Giulia sat motionless, cheek resting against the rock. The stillness in her heart whispered softly in the leaves and flowed down from heaven with the moonlight. The Madonna's solemn smile, forever willing to take on the pain of the world, redeemed the sound of howling alarms and roaring planes. At last the dullness that had made Giulia's memory bearable tore soundlessly, like silk.

The quiet still hung in the clearing around the grotto when Giulia had found her way back to the valley. It fed the Madonna's unwavering smile and smoothed the stern silhouette of her gown. And the courage that Giulia, cradling the broken Jesus child in her arms, had once so urgently called for sat in the space above the Madonna's empty lap.

Speaking Ashes

A Sleeper in the Minefield

When I think back to Kizimbani, I inevitably think of Djazia. It was always as if, with Djazia, the village somehow lived on, buzzing with life and the laughter of children. In my memory I see Kizimbani the way it was when I was growing up, with women chatting amiably at the well while keeping their toddlers from waddling off to their deaths. Maybe it is a way of keeping my mind free from juju, from the madness that I dread like nothing else. The madness of the survivor. For Djazia, like me, still lived somewhere in the void between minefields that is Angola, and only yesterday did I learn of her death. But Kizimbani now is nothing but a curse I can't shake off, a spectre haunting my memory, laughing in my face with blackened teeth.

Only two beings on God's earth remembered Kizimbani. One was Djazia. The other is me. I will tell you this story today, meu caro, to pass on memory, because when Kizimbani burned, the world's order was turned upside down. I left the void of war and came here, only to be thrown into the void gaping within myself. The only string to anchor me, the only thread reaching into this emptiness, was Djazia.

*

But I should start at the beginning, for you, meu caro, know little of Africa or Angola, and little of the way we Herero understand the world. I was born in the municipal town of Xangongo in the south of Angola, where my father worked as a shoemaker, but when I was still a toddler my parents moved to the nearby village of Kizimbani where my mother had grown up. When we arrived there, we found that a fever caused by the South African army poisoning the wells had taken its toll among the villagers. Of my mother's family, only her grandmother was still living.

She was a strange woman, of the kind that often seems to be journeying off to another place where no one else can follow. When you asked her a question she would look at you as if you were an imbecile, or she would laugh and walk away. Sometimes she would mock you; another time she would give you a reply taken from a counting rhyme for children. Yet just when you thought there was no use in even trying to get a reasonable word out of her, she would say just the thing that you needed to hear. But it was not always an answer to your question.

Only the children really took to her, and to them she listened with great kindness. Among the village people she was respected and frowned upon in equal measure. As there was no other use for her – she was obviously inhabited by spirits – and as she loved to tell stories, she had become the village nanny. The women, my own mother among them, brought her their toddlers to look after when they had other work to do. Such a woman was Djazia, my great-grandmother.

No one really knew how Djazia had become like that. Some said it had begun with the murder of her sons by the soldiers of the South African army back in the 1970s. Others said that she had always had one foot in the realm of the ancestors and that the death of her husband and family – my mother was the only one left – had just pushed her over the edge. When she was not telling stories she could be seen mumbling and praying with a tattered rosary. My memory starts with sitting at Djazia's feet, eating yam and listening to stories in which she happily mixed ancient gods with saints and talking animals. Since no one had yet told any of us children that they belonged to separate truths, we did not think it odd. We loved Djazia, and the notion that what unsettled the adults was Djazia's jugglery with the order of things only struck me much later. By then no one was left to be intimidated by her, or to listen to her shrewd wisdom.

It was Djazia who gave me my name: Fidele – the faithful one. When my mother protested and pointed out that actually I already had a name, thank you very much, Djazia just chuckled and said that names were fleeting and only faith persistent, at which my mother gave up and went back to work, knowing that from then on I would be Fidele, whether she liked it or not.

'You know, Fidele,' Djazia said to me one day, 'that life is given to you by your creator, and it is in his hands to end it.' I nodded, already used to the suddenness with which I was introduced to this kind of revelation.

'The strange thing is', she continued, her gaze drifting off, 'that the people who claim to know when's a good time to die usually do not seem to follow any of God's commandments. I am wondering why so many believe them anyway. There must be some element in it that I don't understand.'

I stared at her, at a loss. I must have been about nine. 'What do you mean, Ama?' I asked her. 'Are you talking about the SWAPO? But I thought they wanted to free Angola from the invaders. If nobody went to support them, we would be overrun by the South Africans and the UNITA. I learned that in school.' I was one of the few village children who went to school in Xangongo. The fees used up nearly all my father's meagre income.

My great-grandmother eyed me intensely. 'Did you now? Well, then, I suppose they can't be all wrong, can they? I wonder, though, if the South Africans maybe could get rid of the landmines, so that the Herero could plough their fields again. I suppose if we continue like that, soon there will be nobody to overrun, will there, boy?'

I just shrugged, thinking of the meals we villagers lived on which consisted mainly of fish from the river and the vegetables that grew in our garden plots. The animals we kept had to be driven long distances to the river meadows to find them sustenance, since the fields within a five-miles radius were spiked with landmines. Djazia only chuckled and fished for the rosary that half hung out of her apron pocket.

'Never you mind, Fidele,' she said. 'Never you mind an old rag like me. Go to your school and learn your letters and your Portuguese, and when your balls have dropped and the SWAPO comes knocking, then go and fight for the Republic. But always know when's a good time to die, eh?'

'How would I know about that, Ama? You just said it is in the hands of God.'

She looked at me, an expression of utter surprise on her face. 'Did I now? Well, there you go. My memory's like a broken calabash.'

She squatted in the shadow of the tree that grew next to her ramshackle hut and began to move the rosary through her hands. I turned to go, having spotted a playfellow waving at me, sporting a football. And then Djazia muttered something. I did not understand it then, and I still struggle to grasp it now, more than twenty years later.

'Maybe it is not a matter of choosing the time, then,' she said in her typically slow way, as if she had only just discovered these things herself. As if they were bubbling up inside of her, taking her by surprise as well as everyone else. 'But if God sent death to the people, then it must be walking around on earth, no? Like Jesus did. Or these beasts from the Bible, you remember, the ones with the funny names. Behemoth and Leviathan. If he walks among the people, he sure spends quite a lot of time here in Angola. I wonder if one could make him one's ally. Would be a handsome ally to have, eh? More handsome than the fat-arsed officers from the SWAPO, with their airs and graces.'

Those words would turn out to be Djazia's legacy to me. Back then, however, I pretended not to have heard, since even at my young age I had begun to feel an inkling of the exasperation adults sometimes displayed when talking with Djazia. But, like they had, I was learning not to make it too obvious, because she was so full of spirits that they scarcely found room inside her frail little body. One had to make sure not to arouse the spirits' scorn with disrespectful behaviour.

I left her under her tree and went to play football at the edge of the minefield. Even if one of us had actually managed to get hold of a proper ball like those we had seen in Xangongo, we would not have used it. It was too dangerous. So we kicked around our rags and tore our clothes and grew up like any other village children in Angola in the late 1980s.

Our lives were dominated by three things. The first was the fear of the South African soldiers. The second was the travelling preachers who rolled their eyes at us potential sinners, brandished the book of books and demanded conversion in shrill voices. I was scared of their obsession, and to my child's mind the ever ongoing war was also theirs. I spent a lot of time wondering whose side they might be on, since they seemed not particularly interested in either the SWAPO or the South Africans but more in bullying my tribespeople into crawling on their knees until the women tore at their hair and screamed of Sweet Jesus' sacrifice and the men had a haunted look in their eyes.

If Sweet Jesus died on the cross for the sins of humankind, we could continue to live and work in a village that was littered with death. We could go to bed at night knowing that we could be murdered in our sleep by marauding child soldiers who had not been given their pay. And if we could do nothing else for lack of food, schooling and work, when we were old enough we could go to do our bit, to be a warrior of God, to make Jesus' death worthwhile. Yes, meu caro, Fidele trusted in God and loved Sweet Jesus, and he prayed every evening for a safe night's sleep and his father's return from his workshop in Xangongo.

The third thing that constantly lurked on the precipice of my life was that we were neighbours with death. A thin rope was stretched out between the outer row of village huts and the fields. It divided death from the living quite officially. A football that was shot beyond that rope was lost for ever, and its shooter was in for a good whacking by his mates. Beyond the rope lay a wasteland that had not been ploughed for more than ten years. It was that minefield that Djazia walked into shortly after my tenth birthday.

*

It was early evening, and at first nobody paid attention. We were all used to my great-grandmother suddenly wandering the village on a whim, muttering psalms – or something altogether incomprehensible. I was sitting in front of my parents' hut with some of my mates, sharing a bottle of Coca Cola. When we spotted the familiar ragdoll form of Djazia, we waved to her and offered her some Coke, but she only waved back absent-mindedly and shuffled onwards. We giggled at the sight of her headscarf that had come loose and was trailing behind her. She had one hand in her apron pocket where I knew it was grasping the rosary.

I first became alert when I realised that what she carried in the other hand was her rolled-up sleeping mat. She kept walking towards the rope marking the entrance to the field, and I began to notice her air of determination. By the time I had shoved the half-emptied Coke bottle into my friend's lap, scrambled to my feet and started running after her, Djazia was already staggering over the humpy ground of the death field. I stopped dead at the rope and shouted after her with increasing panic, but she neither turned nor answered, just kept walking, sleeping mat in hand.

My shouting roused first my parents, then the rest of the village. The women, led by my mother, embarked on a fruitless mission to lure Djazia back to safety. They begged and threatened and they called upon Sweet Jesus and they shook their fists. But Djazia kept walking as the shouts behind her died away and a helpless silence settled. At the foot of a solitary tree in the middle of the field, Djazia impassively rolled out her mat and settled on it, re-arranging her headscarf and reaching for the rosary. The latter action I merely intuited from the familiar movement of her hands.

As it became clear that she did not intend to return to Kizimbani before dark, the cluster of villagers slowly dissipated. Each retreated to their own hut, some casting each other stunned looks, some women chatting angrily away, my mother among them.

Sleep deserted me that night, and many nights to follow. I thought of my great-grandmother in the minefield and wondered whether the sleep that eluded me visited her instead. Was she able to rest, surrounded by death that could be triggered by a sudden motion, an unconscious twitch of the body reaching down into the earth? I had seen animals ripped apart by landmines, and some of the older people in the village had lost arms or legs when fleeing across those fields from the South Africans, nearly fifteen years ago, before my birth, when Angola had declared its independence. Many had died there. Did their ghosts still haunt the barren grounds? Did they whisper to Djazia in her sleep, about the pain and the pointlessness of it all?

But I am running ahead, meu caro. These were thoughts I did not have until much later. Back then I was ten years old. I had thought myself brave, with the boasting hubris of any boy at my age, fuelled by the swagger and bravado of the SWAPO soldiers stationed in Xangongo. But that night I realised I was not. In fact, I was shitting myself at the thought of doing what Djazia had done. Stupid, I thought, repeating the words of my mother and convincing myself that no one in their right mind would deliberately walk into a minefield. Stupid old woman, I made myself think, to feel safe again in the world as I had come to know it.

The next morning at sunrise, following an unspoken agreement, the villagers assembled at the rope. Djazia was awake – we could see her squatting, rocking back and forth on her heels. She looked over to us, shielding her eyes against the rising sun. When she spotted me, she waved. All eyes were suddenly on me. Still no one had really spoken a word. My mother crossed her arms in front of her breasts, a determined look on her face. 'Call her,' she demanded.

I cleared my throat, avoiding the eyes of my mates who were staring at me as if I was about to perform a miracle. Slowly I raised a hand and waved back, then shouted, 'Ama Djazia. Won't you come back and have breakfast? You have to eat and drink, and soon the sun will be very hot.'

'As if she didn't know that, Fidele,' my mother hissed. 'Can't you come up with something better?'

I turned round to meet the stare of my tribespeople and realised that no one had a clue what to do.

'Ama,' I shouted again, 'please, we are all worried about you.'

My great-grandmother turned her head and looked in my direction. She was too far away for me to make out her expression, but I felt that in her own way she was apologising for having to disappointment me. And I knew then that she would not come back. My mother sighed. The younger children had already got bored and scuttled off to find somewhere more exciting to play.

'We have to call the Chief from Xangongo,' said my father, who was one of the village elders.

The Chief of Kizimbani had not been seen in the village for quite a while, preferring the comforts and – mostly female – company he enjoyed in Xangongo. He left the everyday tasks to his elders and seemed happy enough with this arrangement, having been witness to his wife and two of his children being murdered by the UNITA fif-

140

teen years back. In a sense, he had taken his leave from Kizimbani the same way that Djazia had, only she had not been able to move away from her place of pain except in spirit.

'And do you think the Chief will come and fetch my grandmother from the minefield himself?' my mother asked with a sneer. She did not think highly of the Chief for having deserted Kizimbani when she herself had moved back from the comforts of Xangongo to support what remained of her family.

An approving murmur rose, and my father raised his hands. 'I will send for the Chief,' he said firmly, and the other elders stood up next to him to demonstrate their unity before a palaver could break out. 'My son Fidele will stay here meanwhile and watch the field. If she moves, Fidele, you will try to make her stay where she is, do you hear me?'

I nodded, feeling numb. I looked over to Djazia's gaunt form and knew that it was going to be long day.

Djazia never left the field. For seven days she sat on her mat, rocking back and forth and praying with the rosary, while I sat under the trees at the village edge, shelter from the glaring midday sun, and found my lips moving together with her hands.

My father came back without the Chief but with an instruction to send someone into the field to fetch her if she would not come out of her own accord. Also, he brought the news of new fights north of Xangongo, and the rumour of scattered UNITA guerrilla battalions roaming the land bordering our municipality. The men started to sharpen their machetes and clean out their guns if they had them. Suddenly the world grew even smaller than it had been, our focus on only two things: following the news from Xangongo and pondering the problem of Djazia. My people were angry with the old woman for causing them trouble when they had far more pressing matters to attend to. It was the duty of everyone to look after the tribe's welfare. You had to make sure that your own needs did not become more important than caring for your neighbours and relatives.

This was never as obvious as when our little village assembled for council. It was early evening again, the sun diving down behind the distant mountains with a velocity you will only ever witness at the equator. My father had returned from his workshop in Xangongo and the elders were raising the question of what was to be done about Djazia. It was her fourth day in the minefield and, though she seemed well enough from a distance, it was clear that soon thirst would seriously affect her.

A spirit of unrest meandered through Kizimbani. I had been used to people going about their business in an unconcerned way, making the best of what they had though it wasn't much, and being grateful that the Herero had not been blighted by assaults or disease for a long while. But today I sensed fear, and at its core lay Djazia's strange and self-absorbed endeavour. The elders found themselves in a serious dilemma. It was their responsibility to ensure that every member of the tribe was taken care of, but at the same time it was hardly possible to ask any member of the tribe to walk into the field of death on a mission to rescue a woman who had voluntarily stepped out of her circle of protection.

In the end, the elders – with the village's consent, for want of a real alternative – agreed to postpone the question of Djazia's rescue until she was in a really serious state, and decided to see whether hunger or thirst would prove an ally and lure her back to safety.

But as you can imagine, meu caro, it did not happen like that. Djazia did not come back to Kizimbani, nor did our chief. What kept trickling in were more rumours of fighting and chaos from the north. Their reality was tangible in the absence of the preachers who had always come at this time of year. I think my father had secretly hoped the preachers would turn up as a kind of panacea and apply their compelling knack of speech to the woman who had turned Kizimbani's order upside down.

It was reluctantly that I went to school, accompanying my father to Xangongo each morning. Thinking back, I think it must have been the fact that my mind was occupied by Djazia that kept me from noticing the growing sense of unrest. Soldiers lurked everywhere, more than usual, dozing in the shadows of the trees fringing the streets, and when we were entering the centre my father would take my hand – something I cannot remember him having done since I was a toddler.

When I came back in the afternoons I would quickly eat the food my mother had ready for me and then dart off to the rope at the village edge. After a couple of days, Djazia and I had developed a routine. When she saw me coming across the sun baked ground she would raise a hand in greeting, and I would wave back, before I settled under the trees facing the minefield. My silhouette in the shadow was a mirror to her fragile form under the other tree out there facing my own. I would see her watching me for a while, and I had a peculiar but certain feeling that she was pleased to see me. My playfellows soon got bored of my being so preoccupied with my mad kinswoman that I would fall asleep under that tree and have to be fetched home by my father. After a few fruitless attempts to interest me in a game of football or a swim, the other boys left me to my strange obsession, hoping I would get back to normal in my own good time. There was a spell cast over Kizimbani. And I was the one most entranced.

*

If you ask me, meu caro, why I was so transfixed by the old woman in the minefield, I will find it very hard to answer. My love for Djazia was one reason. But it was not the only one. I wanted to find out why she was doing it.

During these few weeks that seemed to stretch out into eternity, Djazia became the centre of my world, a fixed idea that mesmerised me and yet that I could not fill with meaning. She sat there, day in, day out, praying with her rosary or just staring into the distance. She never moved one iota from her sleeping mat. As dusk settled she would curl up into a frail but tight little ball and go to sleep. All the while, I was trying to figure out why I had to be there with her, witness to her madness, her biased ally, half fascinated, half repelled. At night I dreamt about doing the unthinkable. In my dream I would lift the rope and slip underneath it.

Like all boys, I was obsessed with bravery. I had had other dreams in the past, in which I marched with the SWAPO or fought as a guerrilla in the mountains. I had a gun in those dreams, and a feeling of being needed. I knew I had killed many, and I was proud of it. But those had been daydreams and had not held this new cold edge of fear.

One morning, Djazia did not rise from her mat but remained curled up on her side without moving. On this day I refused to go to school and my father just patted my shoulder, saying that he would go and fetch the Chief. Someone had to go into the minefield and bring back the old woman. With a sigh he said he feared it was to be him. My mother's hands flew to her mouth and for once she was lost for words. I went back to my tree and stared at Djazia's lifeless form. I wondered if she was dead. But I somehow knew she wasn't.

In the evening, my father returned in a Land Rover, the Chief in the back. Fires were lit, and drums carried to the village square. My tribe called upon the ancestors. There was little room for Sweet Jesus on this night that would decide who was going to live and whose time it was to die. Limbs swayed in the light of the fires, and heads rolled from side to side. My father sat next to the Chief. His face was set and stern. It looked like one of the carved masks the dancers had conjured from the depths of their huts. As my people waited for dawn to bring a turn of tides and lift the enchantment Djazia had cast, I found my way to the edge of the field. As I lifted the rope I was no longer afraid.

My feet touched the hostile ground like a caress. It felt like walking on silky sand. The light of the fires did not reach into my darkness. I could hardly see the path I followed – and had followed in my dreams many nights previously. A curious euphoria filled me. I lost my sense of time. I, Fidele, in this moment became one with my walking. Meu caro, it is hard to describe what brought me through the minefield unharmed. I wonder whether you have ever heard of firewalkers? I learned about this rite only when I came to Europe, but when I saw photographs of people, men and women, walking over red hot coals I felt a strange surge of kinship. There are tribes in the vast folds of Africa that crawl over fire on their bellies and rub their gums with glowing embers. They say you have to become the fire. They say you have to give up all ideas of a divide. I think on this night I became the minefield. My twitching feet felt the danger and carried me past.

Djazia was lying on her mat, curled up as I had last seen her. My eyes had adjusted to the darkness by then and I could see her narrow chest softly rising and falling. For a moment, I just stood there, looking, and taking in the fact that I had made it. Then my great-grandmother opened her eyes.

'Here you are at last, Fidele,' she said.

'Here I am, Ama.'

She nodded, satisfied. She was alarmingly thin; her arms stuck out from her body like knotty twigs. I offered her some water I had brought, and she took it and sipped it in little gulps.

'Come and sit by me, Fidele,' she said. 'I am very tired.'

Suddenly, my knees gave way, and I curled up at her side, and I cried and cried while Djazia stroked my shoulder and whispered words of comfort in voice that was coarse from a week of not speaking. When my tears had finally dried up, I drifted into sleep, my head resting on Djazia's bony thigh. And then the enchantment broke, and hell descended on Kizimbani.

*

I awoke when Djazia gently shook me. Screams echoed on the brink of my consciousness. I rubbed my eyes, trying to get rid of the blurred curtain of red that filled my vision. As I sat up I took in twitching human silhouettes that bounced between the huts in the bizarre manner of moths. Screams of terror rose over Kizimbani and were carried over the field. I saw the fire in the square leaping and licking at the nearest huts. I saw dark men in heavy boots and heard the shots and saw my people helplessly tumbling into the fire or twitching on the ground. I saw shadow machetes flashing down and heard cries muffled by the silky swish of a blade. When all voices had died, and the South Africans had left heaps of limbs and rolling heads as an offering to the fire, all that remained was the angry hissing of the flames. Even that died eventually. In me and around me was a hollowness bereft of all sound.

*

When I think of Kizimbani, I inevitably think of Djazia. I think back to that dark, flame-filled night, the entrancing song of the drums, and the boy whose feet became one with the minefield. For the briefest of times then I had been aligned with death, and death had spared me. And I know I am not brave. I am not brave at all.

Orchard of Stones

1984

The gate stands out against the leaves of the wood. It is half un-hinged, out of place. Bobo sees the star only as she squeezes through the narrow gap, her six-year-old body, as always, ahead of her thoughts. The star has six points and looks like two triangles placed on top of each other. Bobo looks again at her discovery from within and turns to seek the wall that would give meaning to an iron gate in the forest. There is no wall or fence. Only rows of bushes and trees that form a sheltered orchard in the heart of the woods.

But there are the stones. They are square slabs, spread out evenly over the grassy space like the compartments in Mama's ice cube tray that Bobo likes to fill for freezing. She never manages without spill-ing water. On each slab are placed a number of pebbles of all shapes and sizes.

Bobo jumps from stone to stone and plays 'Don't Tread on the Gap'. She counts the slabs. She is not enjoying it. Somehow she knows that she shouldn't be walking over the stones. Somehow, she feels uneasy.

Dusk is falling fast, in spite of the bright late-summer glow. Bobo sits down beneath the gate with its strange star and does not know why she is staying. She should go home. It is late. Mama will be wor-ried. A soft wind ruffles the leaves above her head. It sounds as if somebody is whispering to her in a language she does not under-stand.

1933

Louise wakes up to the sound of splintering glass. It is a piercing noise that reaches deep into her sleep, forming a gaping mouth. The scream is too high-pitched to be human. People are running in the streets. Louise can hear the noise of nailed boots and breathless chanting. Instantly, she knows that some of her college friends are out there with the crowd. They are leaving their books behind to burn somebody else's. Darkness outside; its boundary the neat garden hedge of the vicarage. On the other side an inferno has broken out. Louise sees the shadow of flames dancing on her lace curtains. She blindly fumbles for her dressing gown and staggers to the window.

The printer's shop opposite the vicarage is burning. Fire is leaping out of the broken window front and is already licking at the neighbouring houses, hungry for more. The old timberwork is creaking and bending. Women are running down the stairs, barefoot, screaming for water. Three SA youngsters are standing by, swaying on their feet. Are they drunk? They are watching the scene with blank expressions, apparently unaffected by the general distress. The printer's wife is shaking her fists at them and shouting something incomprehensible. This finally catches their attention. One of them steps forward and hits the woman hard in the face.

'Wash out your mouth, you Jewish bitch!' he bellows.

She holds her face, sobbing, her little son clinging to her legs.

Louise sees her neighbours running for water, coming down the stairs with buckets and saucepans, spilling the precious liquid in their panic. At last, Louise snaps out of her stupor. She runs down the stairs and straight into her brother, Rudolph, who is fully dressed. She can't make out his face in the darkness, only the white dog collar above the lines of his suit.

'Rudi,' she says, her voice breathless. 'Rudi, you must call the fire brigade.'

He takes her by the shoulders, firmly. 'They will not come, Lu.'

'But it's a fire, Rudi. It's a fire. It's a fire.' She is repeating the same line over and over again, like an incantation, to make him listen.

He tightens his grip and shakes her a little. 'They will not come.'

Louise sees her mother at the bottom of the stairs, her long silver braid snaking down her cotton-clad back; silent and wide-eyed, but her mouth as firm and set as Rudi's.

Somebody is hammering at the door. They are calling for the Vicar to come out, to bring back God, to do *something*. But God has averted his eyes. Rudi exchanges one glance with his mother, then silently retreats into his study, where the curtains are drawn.

Her mother places a hand on Louise's shoulder, her touch kinder then her face. 'Go back to bed, pet.'

'There is a fire,' Louise says, helplessly.

1984

Mama and Papa are having a row. It always follows the same pattern. Papa shouts, and Mama answers back calmly at first, trying to be reasonable, reminding him to mind his manners. When Papa shouts like this, it is because he is upset. There are some things that make him upset immediately. One of them is when people mention the war.

Bobo doesn't really know what war is. She understands that it happens when people don't agree with each other. What she does not understand is the bit with the Jews. That is the reason why Papa is shouting and Mama grows all cold and icy and leaves the room and refuses to listen. Papa opens the window and lights a cigarette. He doesn't look at Bobo.

'I've never seen a Jew,' Bobo said to Mama earlier, when Mama explained about the Orchard of Stones. It is Jews that are buried there, but Bobo finds that odd because there are no names, and no real gravestones. It is not a proper graveyard at all.

'Maybe they want to be remembered by something else,' Mama says.

The inside of Bobo's stomach lurches when Mama explains about the camps. Bad people did something horrible to the Jews, a long time ago, when Mama's own mother was young. They all died. Or most of them.

'How?' Bobo asks. She is horrified and curious at the same time, her imagination sparked. Mama looks at Bobo's baby sister, who is playing on the floor, then at back at Bobo. She knows that Bobo will insist now and that she has to be firm not to give in.

'In a very cruel way,' she finally answers. 'Leave it now, Bobo. I don't want you to have nightmares.'

But Bobo isn't willing to give up yet. There is layer of darkness there, something that fascinates her, something that shifts the sun-

149

shine outside, and the bees and the bales of straw and the full su-
permarkets, the clean streets and the books she is learning to read,
books about little girls that love their horses and have best friends
and nice homes where they eat cornflakes and drink cocoa.

Since she is not getting anywhere with the Jews, Bobo starts to
ask about the war. And though Mama explains about soldiers and
fighting and planes that throw bombs and destroy cities, Bobo can
see that Mama is not telling her everything.

'Can you remember the war?'

'No,' Mama says. Mama was born when the war was already over.
'But Papa can,' she adds, cautiously. 'And Grandmama Louise.'

Papa comes in and picks up Bobo's little sister, casting a glance at
Bobo, flushed with excitement, and at his wife, who seems a little
out of sorts.

'We are talking about the Jews,' Bobo declares, with the sobriety
that she thinks befits the occasion.

'Are you now?' Papa says flatly.

'Mama says they were all killed by bad Germans,' Bobo contin-
ues, proud that she is now educated on the matter. Then she adds,
pleased to share her discovery with Papa, 'But I have found the place
where they have gone.'

'They are dead now, Bobo,' says Mama. 'Or they have gone away
from Germany. I have told you, it is a cemetery. People are buried
there.'

Bobo gets impatient. They do not understand.

'But they are still there,' she insists. 'They haven't left. They are in
the stones.'

Mama's face suddenly twists and she begins to cry. Bobo falls silent, shocked. Mama's tears make her world tumble far more than
wars or dead Jews. Bobo's sister, too, starts crying and kicks her father, wanting to be set down. Bobo turns to Mama and hugs her legs.

This is when the shouting begins.

1945

Pius hears the bombers before they come into sight. His friends hear
them too, and they start running. The street is deserted. It is an unu-

sually warm March afternoon. Except for the six little boys, everybody is inside to escape the heat. They are on their way back from school, kicking a football to each other. The ball belongs to Pius; it is his birthday present and he is eager not to let it out of sight. He shouts to the others. They should bloody wait for him while he ties his shoelaces, and it is *his* ball. But they just laugh as they get covered in dust.

When the air raid alarm starts, the bombers have already dived through the clouds. They are flying so low, Pius can see the propellers spinning. He flings himself into the doorway of the bakery and, through the glass, looks at the frozen figure of the baker's daughter who is working the tills this afternoon.

He sees his friends running, one by one throwing away their satchels to be free of the weight. The first detonation sends dust and stone flying everywhere. Two shops down the street the glass falls out of the windows, almost silently, the splintering drowned by the roaring of the planes. The impact is so close that Pius's world goes silent.

Momentarily deafened, he doesn't hear the screaming behind him, only feels the door opening as the baker's girl tries to drag him inside.

When the dust has settled, nobody is running. There are five little heaps on the ground further along the road. None of them moves. The only thing moving is the football rolling towards Pius, bouncing off the pavement, rolling here and there, aimlessly.

1934

Rudi is angry. Not with Louise, not with their mother, but with God. Rudi sometimes just is. It is the burden of the intelligent, his friend says, the one who looks at Louise a little too long and a little too often. Louise is never angry with God. In fact, she does not understand what God has to do with the matter of Father's pension. It is the pension that she and her mother should be living on and which the new government refuses to pay. There has been another letter today and Rudi is fuming.

'What the hell do they mean, "not entitled to the money of German tax payers"?' He waves the paper in front of his mother's kind but worn-out face.

'You know what they mean,' she says, tired of his ranting that is not going to get them the pension, not going to get them back their house, not getting them anything but trouble.

'And you should know your place, Rudi. As you have done until now.'

'But he built a bloody railway for them!' Rudi shouts. 'Didn't care he was French back then, did they?'

'He is gone now,' Louise says suddenly.

Both mother and brother look at her, surprised.

'He is gone,' she repeats. 'They can't hurt him. But they can hurt us. If we are French, that is not too bad, is it? Not too bad. Let them leave it at that.'

Her mother and Rudi exchange a look, and then the older woman nods. Rudi looks at Louise with a tenderness he does not often show.

'There will be no money then, Lu. You will have to leave college.'

Louise looks down at her hands. They can write beautifully, those hands. They can write German and French very well, and some English. She always wanted to learn more English. She places one hand on top of the other, carefully. She will have to leave it at that.

'I'll keep house for you,' she says. 'Then you can let go of the maid. She is too nosy, anyway.'

Rudi takes both her hands in his for a moment and squeezes hard.

'It is a shame,' he says quietly. 'A shame.'

Louise pulls away. She does not want to think or talk now. She has made up her mind.

'There is worse,' she says.

Louise is never angry with God.

1955

The heat makes everybody drowsy. In the evenings, Mona's aunt and uncle light lanterns on the lawn and everyone gathers round the garden table for dinner. Mona is too hot and also far too excited to eat much. Uncle Albert wears a shawl over his shoulders and a funny round cap on his head. Aunt Eloise looks like she always looks, but they all sing strange and beautiful songs in a language that is not French. Even the boys join in, who always say singing is for babies. Mona is eight, and she is sometimes homesick.

Once a week she is allowed to phone home to Germany. Her mother asks her about her adventures, about Uncle Albert, who is her mother's cousin, about Aunt Eloise and their boys. Is Mona making progress with her French? Does she pray at night? Is she not giving Auntie and Uncle too much trouble? The last question sounds rather worried. In her family, Mona is called 'Holy Terror' because she tends to run away and sometimes sneaks out of Sunday school to go to the ice cream parlour.

'The French are a bit strange,' Mona says on the phone to her mother.

Her mother laughs. 'Indeed. And why is that, darling?'

'Because they celebrate Mass on Fridays.'

There is a pause on the other end.

'Mama?' Mona asks.

Her mother is silent for another moment before she answers. 'Well, maybe they are a bit strange, after all. They do lots of things differently in France.'

'They sing all kind of songs that are not French at all, and they never cook or clean on Saturdays. They have a maid who comes in for that. I don't know why they pay a maid to do it then when Auntie does it herself the rest of the week. Sometimes they even work on Sundays.'

'I guess your auntie needs a bit of a break sometimes too,' Mama says, but she sounds slightly worried now.

Oh no, Mona thinks. *Now she will ask me whether they go to church.* She has not told Mama that she has not been to church since she arrived here. She is very certain this would alarm her mother more than anything. Mona, for her part, thinks that missing church is the best part of the holiday.

'Listen, Mona,' her mother says, putting on her sternest voice. 'Be good and give Auntie a hand and say your prayers at night. But before you go can you get me Uncle Albert for a moment?'

Mona blows her mother a kiss, as she always does and which

Mama never returns, and calls for Uncle Albert. He comes into the hall, slow and cheerful, and takes up the phone.

'Well, my dear Louise,' he says in his forever pleasant manner. What follows is a monologue by her mother, in rapid French, while Uncle's cheerfulness drops like the temperature at night. He waves to Mona to go and play outside and turns his back on her.

Later that day, which is a Friday, there is no singing and no funny cap at dinner.

'Don't we celebrate Mass today?' Mona asks in her patchy French. She is a little disappointed, since she had started to like their little ritual together, even though she could never make sense of it.

The table falls silent, and the boys, who usually wolf down any food they are presented with, push the salad around on their plates. Aunt and Uncle exchange a glance, and then Uncle Albert smiles at her. 'Not today, sweetheart.'

Auntie Eloise reaches over and ruffles Mona's hair. 'Your Mama says we shall get you to church on Sunday. We don't want you to become a little heathen, hmm?'

Mona looks from one to another. 'No,' she says, tentatively. Suddenly, she wishes she hadn't mentioned any of it to her mother. Now she will have to go to church, and it will be as dull and long as in Germany, only more so, because she will not be able to understand half the words.

As she looks up again she wonders why, still, no one is eating.

1984

'Why did you cry earlier?' Pius asks Mona after the children have gone to bed. They are in their own bedroom, lying side by side, and feeling like strangers as they have done a lot these last few years. Mona does not feel like sharing her grief with Pius just now, not after he shouted at her and accused her of indoctrinating their daughter. *This is the thing with Pius*, Mona thinks. *When it comes to the war, he just won't think straight*. Mona is always afraid that someone might mistake Pius for a fascist. She has lost count of the occasions when she has felt embarrassed for him. Whenever someone speaks of the Holocaust he gets angry to the point of losing control.

'I refuse to be made guilty for something I haven't done,' he shouts at whoever is there to listen.

'And anyway, what of Dresden, what of all the German civilians, what of the men who died in the work camps or made it home as emotional wrecks?'

Nobody speaks about the war when Pius is around, unless they don't know any better. And now Bobo has sparked the latest row in the line of their disagreement on all this.

'Are you not going to answer me?' Pius asks, sullen.

'No,' Mona says waspishly, 'because if I do you will shout at me again. And I've had enough of that today, thanks.'

Pius shrugs. 'It's just because of all this idiocy,' he says. 'They are trying to make the children feel guilty and responsible, left, right and centre, taking away the last scraps of their identity. I will not let you do the same to our girls.'

Mona has had enough of this, enough of things being so complicated.

'Bobo stumbled upon a Jewish cemetery. Of course I will tell her the truth.'

'Will you indeed? And what is the truth? Pray tell me that. Is Bobo old enough to understand the truth, the whole of it?'

'You can't deny what happened back then,' Mona hisses. Sometimes, she truly hates him for making her feel so completely wrong in herself, so much in the wrong in everything she thinks or says.

'It all happened, and it is terrible. And yes, I feel guilty about it.'

'Then they have brainwashed you as well,' Pius says.

Mona looks at him in shock. 'I wish I knew why you are like this. What has made you think like this? You speak of forgiving ourselves, and having belief in our history, and not defining ourselves by what happened forty years ago. And yet you can't bear me speaking about it, telling Bobo nothing but the truth. You can't even forgive me for feeling different from you.'

Pius folds his arms and regards Mona. 'There is nothing wrong with me,' he says, his mouth set. 'I just see clearly that this whole guilt trip is just as much propaganda as they used to advocate Hitler's war.'

'And to what effect, may I ask?'

'To make us all wobbly, like jelly. We are the most wishy-washy nation in Europe when it comes to anything beyond being efficient and punctual. The only thing we are known for these days is the Oktoberfest. Isn't that fantastic? A thorough job, I would say.' Pius's voice drips with irony.

'Nobody to blame but us alone.'

'What would you know, anyway? You hadn't even been born.'

Mona sits up. She is going to tell him now. Now is as good as anytime.

'I think my mother is Jewish.'

Pius stares at her, blankly. Then he says, 'Have you now lost it completely?'

Mona shakes her head. 'I think she was from a Jewish family. In France. I remember them from when I was a child. They celebrated the Sabbath. On a Friday. And no one worked on Saturdays. There are other clues as well.'

Pius shakes his head in disbelief. 'Your mother is as Catholic as the Pope.'

Mona nods, slowly. 'Yes. And so was her mother. But her father wasn't. He never did go to church.'

'Her brother was a minister!'

'They never spoke about the war. Or what happened to her French relatives, her father's family.'

'Your family has never been one for speaking the truth,' Pius says. 'They like to keep up appearances at all costs, don't they? That's why they didn't come to our wedding. Didn't like the idea of their daughter marrying a working-class boy.'

'What has that got to do with this?'

'Everything.'

Mona can feel the tears coming, pricking hot behind her eyelids. She fights against the urge to cry. She doesn't want to be vulnerable again, even though it is the only thing that will pacify him. He hates it when she is cold, and unattainable, because it reminds him of her mother. But she believes he is in the wrong. She will not let him have that victory.

'Go and talk to her about it,' Pius says.

'I can't.'

'Why not?'

'She will never admit it.'

'Well, maybe because it's ridiculous.'

'It is not. Believe me. She hates to speak about the past. It is almost as if certain things had not happened, in her world. Whenever she speaks about that time, it's as if she only reveals snapshots. Never the whole picture. Never how she felt, or what happened to her. I remember my father mentioning once that she was bullied by checkpoint soldiers because she had a French name. He joked and said it was the only reason she married him. But Ma looked at him as if she wanted to scuff out his eyes.'

Pius settles down beside her again, calmer now, and less defensive. 'I would be surprised if it were true, Mona. How would she have managed to conceal it, all that time, what with her French ancestry and all?'

'She *did* get married, didn't she? Nobody would have noticed then.'

'Even so.'

Mona is not convinced and regrets having told Pius in the first place. He rarely understands her these days.

'Is that why you were crying earlier?' he asks.

She nods but does not answer.

'Talk to her,' he tells her again.

If only his tone wasn't so smug and self-righteous, I would accept it as an offer of peace, an attempt to support me. But it's always just about him being right, in the end, about speaking the truth, and so I can't.

'I can't,' Mona says.

'Then you are no better than her.' Pius can barely conceal his disappointment.

'No, I am not. You're right. There, are you happy now?'

He takes it personally, as if she was refusing to talk to him as well. Even though she has tried. Has been trying for years.

'When I was a child I was a rebel,' she says, as astonished about this fact as if it concerned another child, another life.

'Pity I didn't know you then.' He turns to the wall, pulling the blanket over him.

And now the tears come. Mona wipes them away in silence. She is glad that Pius has switched off the lights and that this time his victory will go unnoticed.

1934

Louise cuts out a star from a paper napkin and pins it to her blouse. It crumples at the ends immediately. The real ones are made of cloth, of course. People stitch them on, for neatness's sake. In the mirror her skin looks yellow, like the paper. She thinks her star looks almost like a Girl Scout's badge, two triangles orderly placed on top of each other, as if she was committed to a good cause. She hears her brother's footsteps outside and hastily rips the paper from her chest, tearing a hole in her silk blouse.

'Are you coming, Lu?' her brother shouts from downstairs.

Outside, the bells begin to toll, calling people to Mass. Louise changes her blouse. It is as easy as that. They will never know. They will never find out.

1946

Pius stands in the hallway, eavesdropping. There is no sound, so he stands back again from the door, which is half ajar. His mother must have left, gone to the neighbours or to visit her sister, as she always does when the silence becomes unbearable. Pius's sisters and brothers have gone into town – the younger ones to play, the older ones for drinks or to see their sweethearts. They are all old enough to escape if they want.

Pius, at seven, is the youngest. He is the one who carries the silence if no one is left in the house with his father, who is now sitting in his favourite armchair. He hasn't left it for three days. The lounge is gloomy, mostly because his father doesn't care to turn on the light. It blinds him, he says. He has been very sensitive to light ever since he suffered snow blindness in Russia. As he sits by the window he sucks on his pipe. The smoke is curling up in the dusky air to form strange elaborate patterns.

'Come in, Pius,' Father says.

Pius obeys. He is a very compliant child, as his mother never fails to tell the neighbours. He doesn't leave the house much these days, even though there are no air raids anymore.

'Do you want a cup of something, Father?'

The man in the chair, who looks about ten years older than he is, shakes his head.

'No, lad. Come and sit awhile with your father. Do you want me to tell you a story?'

Pius wants neither to sit with his father or to listen to his stories. His father's stories are about people dying in trenches, about limbs falling off without their owners noticing, and about camps surrounded by barbed wire. They are graphic and detailed and they give Pius nightmares.

Pius doesn't know what he dreads more: the times when his father falls into a stupor and neither speaks not looks at anyone, or when he spills out the horror piled up inside him. Pius feels bad because he wants to run away from this stranger whom he only remembers from blurry, brief visits: a hulk in uniform who stuffed himself with Mother's cooking and then vanished again to an obscure task that no one ever explained to Pius.

Now his father doesn't wear a uniform, and he is skinny and haggard even though he always gets the biggest portion of each meal.

'The doctor says it is important that he speaks about his experience,' Pius's mother repeats frequently, like the neighbour's parrot. His father, she says, is lucky enough to have a doctor who is forward thinking.

'If he speaks about it,' she said, 'it will get better soon. He will get a job and we will have some money. Then you can join the football club and the library.'

His father hasn't got a job yet, he still has a bad cough and his skin is raw and oozing from the frostbite he got in Russia. But he does speak, and mostly to Pius.

'Listen to him,' Mother said. 'Promise you will listen to him.' Pius has promised.

'Come in, lad,' his father says again. He sounds more impatient now. Pius comes in and sits on the edge of the sofa. Dusk is falling quickly now and the room is slowly sinking into darkness.

'Have I told you about the day when we went into the forest to cut trees and some of the other buggers escaped? They nearly shot us then, all of us. Imagine, Pius, if they'd shot all of us. I wouldn't be here then. Have I told you about that?'

'No, Father.'

'Your old man has been on some dangerous adventures, I tell you. Would you like to go on an adventure like that? Would you, Pius?'

Pius doesn't answer, but it goes on from there anyway. Pius knows all about the camps, all about the Russians and the killing. With every story, there are more details that make Pius feel sick, make him want to run away and hide and read *The Jungle Book*, which is waiting on his bedside table.

'A man needs a son to tell the tale,' his father says. 'The others don't give a damn about their old man, little hypocrites, don't care that I went out there to fight for the ungrateful lot of them. But you are different, Pius. You respect your father. Have I told you about the day when I had to use my knife to cut off this Russian chap's boots because they were frozen to his feet? Isn't that funny? Have you ever been so cold, Pius? I bet you haven't.'

Pius sits and listens. He sits quietly and patiently while his father spoon-feeds him the horror in neat mouthfuls. Sometimes, when it is over, Pius wishes that one could throw up words, purge them out of one's system and drain them down the toilet. Instead he feels them piling up inside, growing like an ulcer, and he knows that they will spill out again, one day, and wash over the world like a tide of toxic bile.

1947

Ice has come in the place of bombs and fire. Ice and hunger. The Rhine has frozen over, the war is lost and the world has stopped. There are blue faces and skinny limbs in the lines where people queue for supplies. Louise queues for hours on end. She can hardly bear to look at the children. Little Mona, snug and warm under Louise's winter coat, has rosy skin and is sleeping, tiny fists clenched, while Louise listens to the stories of people in Berlin freezing to death in the debris of their houses. There is hardly any food. In the queues, Louise hears stories of refugee treks, of thousands of homeless people, of children starving alone in fields that are barren.

Louise is cooking soup with cabbage, water and pearl barley. The American soldiers are mostly good, almost jovial. They try to give her nine-year-old daughter chocolate and canned beef and do not ask her for food stamps.

'Excuse me', Louise says in her awkward English. 'Excuse me. We not need charity. My husband works for the new ministry, you know.'

The man shoves the chocolate bar back in his pocket, suddenly dismissive. 'You all need charity, Missus,' he says, with only a hint of disgust. 'Though, by God, you don't deserve it.'

The man looks at the tattered crowd before him, the tired, chiselled faces returning his gaze with blankness. He wants to challenge them, wants them to answer back. Nobody speaks. Their words have frozen over like the river.

1994

Louise wakes up in her hospital bed and longs for her youngest daughter. But as she turns her head it isn't Mona she sees, but her older sister.

'What is it, Ma?' Her daughter puts aside the book she is reading.

Louise closes her eyes. She opens her mouth and tries to ask for Mona, but there is no sound. Louise is not surprised. How would there be, after all this time? Her memories are like a garden in which all the flowers have turned to stone, their essence locked for ever in a smooth shell: inaccessible, unspoken. Louise feels their weight on her chest, a whole quarry of them. The doctors say there is nothing wrong with her really. It is the depression that makes her heart weak and her life seep away.

'I wish the Good Lord would take me,' Louise whispers, startling her daughter, who had just begun reading again.

'Don't be silly, Ma. You'll be right as rain soon. Just try and be a little more cheerful, will you? Look, the sun is shining.'

But Louise doesn't care about the sun anymore. The sun can't make her stone flowers grow. She wants to leave this orchard of stone and go to another garden where she will be forgiven. She has been a good and dutiful Christian. She has taken the Holy Communion every Sunday without fail, and so have her daughters. She has been as truthful as she can. She has to be forgiven.

'Will I be forgiven?' she asks Mona when her youngest daughter comes to visit the next day.

'Yes,' Mona replies without hesitation.

'How can you be sure?' Louise whispers, clinging to the younger woman's words.

Mona thinks for a while. 'Because you have tried to do what is right.'

'Is that enough?'

'No one can do more than that.'

'I wish you hadn't got divorced,' Louise replies before she slips back into sleep.

Driving back home, Mona wonders whether she has told her mother a lie, whether trying is as good as doing right and whether everyone is obliged to use the voice that is given to them. A whole generation of the guilty is dying in this decade, tormented by the same questions. A generation of fascists, hacks, cowards, the igno-rant and those who averted their eyes.

Mona stops the car and walks down to the river.

It is spring and there is life everywhere. In the water meadows outside the city some people brave the chill and swim in the shallow water by the shore. Mona thinks of the old photographs of Louise and Rudi in those chaste swimming costumes that reach down to the knees; swimming in the Rhine. Random threads to tie on to when so much of history is torn away.

Mona thinks back to the orchard of stone that her daughter once found in the woods. When does a story end, and where does it begin, when so much of it remains untold? And is a song unheard just be-cause it has not been sung? Maybe, she thinks, some stories grow silently, like trees in the groves of memory, nurtured by those who want to listen. And Mona wonders who will have the voice to tell.

2008

Bobo is sitting in the library doing research for an article, when she hears of her father's passing. At first she thought it was her boss from the publishers and she started talking immediately: she is sorry for the delay, she will write up the article tonight, yes, she is aware of the deadlines, but she has so much to do. Awfully sorry.

'Bobo,' her mother's voice interrupts Bobo's breathless atonement. 'Papa is dead.'

Bobo sits down where she stands.

'You don't need to come right now,' Mama says. 'Do something. Go for a walk. I will ring you when you can see him.' Mama gives Bobo the address of the undertaker and tells her that her father died in the night.

'Why didn't you call me earlier?' Bobo croaks. Her voice sounds faint and unreal, like the news she has just received.

'Every story needs some time to end,' Mama says quietly.

It hasn't really come as a shock to Bobo. Her father has been in hospital for these past six month, suffering from the aftermath of a stroke. Bobo was prepared. But she still feels vulnerable, split open like a shell. After the funeral, she sits in a café with Mama and her younger sister.

'I have something to tell you both,' Mama says. And she tells her daughters what Pius told her, during those last painful weeks, when he could hardly speak anymore but had to rely on his ex-wife to make sense of his stammer. The wife he hadn't spoken to for the past fifteen years. Now Mama passes his story on, with all the details, a woman who has learned to own the truth.

'I had no idea,' Bobo says.

'Neither had I,' says her mother.

'I have no idea what to do with this.'

'Neither have I.'

The three of them fall silent for a while.

'I sometimes think', Mona says pensively, 'that my generation has taken on the pain that our parents could not carry alone. After the war, I mean. After they had proven to the world how effortlessly modern man can turn to the greatest monstrosity, using all his enlightened sophistication to design terror. It was just too much, too overwhelming. It would have crushed them had they given in to it.'

'Tell us more,' Bobo says, firmly, and her sister nods.

Mona sits up straight, as if something has suddenly been lifted from her. When she begins to speak about Louise it sounds as if she has done this many times before.

2011

The last lines are always the most difficult. Only a story with a good ending is worth telling. The last lines often decide whether a story sticks in a reader's memory. Sometimes endings jump out of Bobo's keyboard, ready to align on the page. Sometimes she battles with them, as she does with this one. She has told a story of fragments, misplaced scraps of truth that need a storyteller to piece them together. Whenever Bobo becomes anxious and wonders whether the story is worth telling, she reminds herself that every tale begins with just one splinter of truth that sparks our imagination.

Bobo tends to find stories in places and take them away without stealing them. There are invisible strings that tie her heart to all her story places. Sometimes she feels this gentle tugging inside, and then she remembers. Some are only alive in her memory. Some she has revisited. None of them is forgotten. They wash into Bobo's own story like driftwood, and sometimes it takes a while to make sense of their shapes and forms. Sometimes they spill out on to the page like a strange, outlandish river that Bobo did not even know had formed within.

She builds ornaments of words and links them together in a sudden flash of insight. She does not know where they come from, these memories she finds in places. But she knows that it began in an orchard of stones that was deserted and alive at the same time. It began when she was six years old.

Bobo does not live in the past, but she gathers and keeps the memories she finds with such vehemence that she herself is puzzled sometimes.

Bobo has a deadline to meet and she needs to send her manuscript to her publisher. Only this story does not want to end, because it is part of her own. It is a story like a fragmented garden, its composition fallen to ruin, where meaning can only be found in the detail. You must go and look for it closely. You must find the ghosts of long ago and let them speak.

Maybe this is as good a last line as any.

Acknowledgements

My thanks go out to the following Firekeepers. I would not have been able to finish this book without them:

To Paul E. Crabb, for his amazing artwork.

To Julia Farley, who did a marvellous job of proofreading and type-setting the first edition and must have read the manuscript more times than I have.

To Kevan Manwaring, for friendship, loyalty and inspiration, and for having faith in my voice.

To Anthony Nanson of Awen Publications, editor and friend, for his feedback, meticulous work and thoughtful queries, which have been invaluable in creating an improved edition of this book.

To my tribe of Firekeepers, for being relentless believers in your own flame and mine. You know who you are.

To the members of the Bath Storytelling Circle and the Stroud Prose Group, who listened to my stories mindfully and patiently and gave me much-needed feedback.

To all men, women and children in Europe, Africa and India who have contributed, without knowing, to this book and my own story.

And to my mother, father and sister, a family of Holy Fools, whom I have to thank for a lifetime of faith and support.

www.awenpublications.co.uk

Also available from Awen Publications:

The Long Woman
Kevan Manwaring

An antiquarian's widow discovers her husband's lost journals and sets out on a journey of remembrance across 1920s England and France, retracing his steps in search of healing and independence. Along alignments of place and memory she meets mystic Dion Fortune, ley-line pioneer Alfred Watkins, and a Sir Arthur Conan Doyle obsessed with the Cottingley Fairies. From Glastonbury to Carnac, she visits the ancient sites that obsessed her husband and, tested by both earthly and unearthly forces, she discovers a power within herself.

'A beautiful book, filled with the quiet of dawn, and the first cool breaths of new life, it reveals how the poignance of real humanity is ever sprinkled with magic.' *Emma Restall Orr*

Fiction ISBN 978-1-906900-44-1 £9.99
The Windsmith Elegy Volume 1

Exotic Excursions
Anthony Nanson

In these stories Anthony Nanson charts the territory between travel writing and magic realism to confront the exotic and the enigmatic. Here are epiphanies of solitude, twilight and initiation. A lover's true self unveiled by a mountain mist … a memory of the lost land in the western sea … a traveller's surrender to the allure of ancient gods … a quest for primeval beings on the edge of extinction. In transcending the line between the written and the spoken word, between the familiar and the unfamiliar, between the actual and the imagined, these tales send sparks across the gap of desire.

'He is a masterful storyteller, and his prose is delightful to read … His sheer technical ability makes my bones rattle with joy.' *Mimi Thebo*

Fiction/Travel ISBN 987-0-9546137-7-8 £7.99

Dancing with Dark Goddesses: movements in poetry
Irina Kuzminsky

The dance is life – life is the dance – in all its manifestations, in all its sorrow and joy, cruelty and beauty. And the faces of the Dark Goddesses are many – some are dark with veiling and unknowing, some are dark with sorrow, some are dark with mystery and a light so great that it paradoxically shades them from sight. The poems in this collection are an encounter with many of these faces, in words marked with feminine energy and a belief in the transformative power of the poetic word. Spiritual and sexual, earthy and refined, a woman's voice speaks to women and to the feminine in women and men – of an openness to life, a surrender to the workings of love, and a trust in the Dark Goddesses and their ways of leading us through the dance.

'Potent, seminal, visionary' *Kevin George Brown*

Poetry/Dance ISBN 978-1906900-12-0 £9.99

Words of Re-enchantment: writings on storytelling, myth, and ecological desire
Anthony Nanson

The time-honoured art of storytelling – ancestor of all narrative media – is finding new pathways of relevance in education, consciousness-raising, and the journey of transformation. Storytellers are reinterpreting ancient myths and communicating the new stories we need in our challenging times. This book brings together the best of Anthony Nanson's incisive writings about the ways that story can re-enchant our lives and the world we live in. Grounded in his practice as a storyteller, the essays range from the myths of Arthur, Arcadia, and the voyage west, to true tales of the past, science-fiction visions of the future, and the big questions of politics and spirituality such stories raise. The book contains full texts of exemplar stories and will stimulate the thinking of anyone interested in storytelling or in the use of myth in fiction and film.

'This excellent book is written with a storyteller's cadence and understanding of language. Passionate, fascinating and wise.' *Hamish Fyfe*

Storytelling/Mythology/Environment ISBN 978-1-906900-15-1 £9.99

Iona
Mary Palmer

What do you do when you are torn apart by your 'selves'? The pilgrim poet, rebel Mordec and tweedy Aelia set sail for Iona – a thin place, an island on the edge. It's a journey between worlds, back to the roots of #their culture. On the Height of Storm they relive a Viking massacre, at Port of the Coracle encounter vipers. They meet Morrighan, a bloodthirsty goddess, and Abbot Dominic with his concubine nuns. There are omens, chants, curses … During her stay Mordec learns that words can heal or destroy, and the poet writes her way out of darkness. A powerful story, celebrating a journey to wholeness, from an accomplished poet.

'Always truthful, this poetry confronts both beauty and ugliness and makes space for light to slip between the two.' *Rose Flint*

Poetry ISBN 978-0-9546137-8-5 £6.99 Spirit of Place Volume 1

The Fifth Quarter
Richard Selby

The Fifth Quarter is Romney Marsh, as defined by the Revd Richard Harris Barham in *The Ingoldsby Legends*: 'The World, according to the best geographers, is divided into Europe, Asia, Africa, America and Romney Marsh.' It is a place apart, almost another world. This collection of stories and poems explores its ancient and modern landscapes, wonders at its past, and reflects upon its present. Richard Selby has known Romney Marsh all his life. His writing reflects the uniqueness of The Marsh through prose, poetry, and written versions of stories he performs as a storyteller.

Fiction/Poetry ISBN 978-0-9546137-9-2 £9.99 Spirit of Place Volume 2

Mysteries
Chrissy Derbyshire

This enchanting and exquisitely crafted collection by Chrissy Derbyshire will whet your appetite for more from this superbly talented wordsmith. Her short stories interlaced with poems depict chimeras, femmes fatales, mountebanks, absinthe addicts, changelings, derelict warlocks, and persons foolhardy enough to stray into the beguiling world of Faerie. Let the sirens' song seduce you into the Underworld …

Fiction/Poetry ISBN 978-1-906900-45-8 £8.99

CPSIA information can be obtained
at www.ICGtesting.com
Printed in the USA
LVHW010006240122
709153LV00006B/986